Dear Reader,

I've always loved the craziness of fashion, where the absurd often hangs right next to the sublime. Hmmm—kind of sounds like romantic comedy, doesn't it? Well, how could I resist? I just had to create Gillian Caine, a fashion designer from New York City who has just been dumped and swindled by a definite Mr. Wrong. Gillian was a delight to write. She's strong-willed, creative, independent. She's a girl who intends to stand on her own two feet—even when they're stuffed into a pair of pumps with five-inch heels. To add to the fun, I transplanted Gillian to Timber Bay, Michigan— the small town I first introduced in my June, 2004, Flipside, *Finding Mr. Perfect*. Timber Bay is the kind of place where buying a new flannel shirt every winter is considered keeping up with the latest trends—until Gillian hits town, that is!

Gillian Caine is one of my favorite creations. A real Flipside kind of girl! I hope you have fun getting to know her as she commits *Random Acts of Fashion* on the eccentric citizens of Timber Bay.

May the fashion be with you,

Nikki Rivers

"I want you to decorate the tree with these," Gillian ordered

Lukas nudged the box beside him, then looked at the suspended branches in the shop window. Opening the carton, he sputtered, "These are...um—"

"Lingerie, McCoy. Now get to work!"

"Yes, warden," he grumbled, picking up a violet camisole. He continued arranging the garments as Gillian came over to inspect his work. Not used to her closeness, Lukas tripped over the stool, lunging toward her, crashing through the tree. Bras and panties took flight like a colorful flock of frightened birds.

"Lukas?" Gillian tossed underwear aside until she found a nose sticking out of the leg of a French-cut panty.

"Are you all right?" she asked as she lifted the lingerie. "Not exactly the way it's worn, McCoy," she said, grinning down at him.

"Maybe you'd like to demonstrate the right way to wear it then, warden," he replied, his mouth holding back a wicked grin.

Nikki Rivers

Random Acts of Fashion

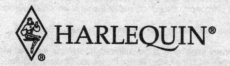

HARLEQUIN®

TORONTO • NEW YORK • LONDON
AMSTERDAM • PARIS • SYDNEY • HAMBURG
STOCKHOLM • ATHENS • TOKYO • MILAN • MADRID
PRAGUE • WARSAW • BUDAPEST • AUCKLAND

ISBN 0-373-44207-6

RANDOM ACTS OF FASHION

ABOUT THE AUTHOR

Nikki Rivers loves writing romantic comedy because she believes that laughter is just as necessary to life as love is. She also gets a kick out of creating quirky characters, having come from a long line of them, herself. Nikki lives in Milwaukee, Wisconsin, with her very own Mr. Right. She loves to hear from readers. E-mail her at RiversWrites@aol.com.

Books by Nikki Rivers

HARLEQUIN FLIPSIDE
17—FINDING MR. PERFECT

HARLEQUIN DUETS
66—A SNOWBALL'S CHANCE

HARLEQUIN AMERICAN ROMANCE
550—SEDUCING SPENCER
592—DADDY'S LITTLE MATCHMAKER
664—ROMANCING ANNIE
723—HER PRINCE CHARMING
764—FOR BETTER, FOR BACHELOR

Don't miss any of our special offers. Write to us at the following address for information on our newest releases.

Harlequin Reader Service
U.S.: 3010 Walden Ave., P.O. Box 1325, Buffalo, NY 14269
Canadian: P.O. Box 609, Fort Erie, Ont. L2A 5X3

To my sisters, Bobbi, Pat, and Judy.
Thanks for the laughter, the strength, and the
love—and for all those bizarre weekends at the
bazaar. Yes! An ant *can* move a rubber tree plant!

1

THE BLACK PICKUP TRUCK with Timber Bay Building and Restoration painted on its side in old-fashioned gold script pulled up to the curb in front of the Sheridan Hotel. Lukas McCoy got out of the driver's seat and slammed the door behind him.

"I should have known," he grumbled, scowling at the workmen installing a sign on one of the storefronts across the street. "Tigers never change their stripes."

His partner and best friend, Danny Walker, got out the passenger side. "Lukas, pal, I never noticed how fond you are of non sequiturs."

Lukas gave Danny a look. "Hannah teach you a new word this morning over toast and coffee?"

Danny grinned. "We skipped breakfast, pal. We're still on our honeymoon."

Danny had married Hannah Ross at the end of the summer. Everyone said it was the most beautiful wedding that Timber Bay had ever seen. And they were thrilled that Hannah, a research sociologist who'd come to Timber Bay on a misguided mission to find the perfect American family for an ad campaign, had stayed to become one of them. But it was still a little weird for Lukas to think of Danny as being married. He'd always figured that Danny would be a lifetime Lothario. Lukas had been the one most likely of the two to settle down with a wife. Danny had been his best friend since grade school and Lukas begrudged him nothing. But damned if he wasn't just a little jealous of Danny's happiness. Facing that satisfied grin of his partner's every morning was starting to get mighty old.

And now this, Lukas thought sourly as he watched the neon sign being put into place in the window of the long-empty shop that used to be known as Clemintine's Frocks.

"The big-city princess should have known to hire a local company, at least. Haven't they ever heard of such a thing as goodwill in New York City? Don't they know that it's important to do business with somebody local? And just look at that. Neon." Lukas spat out the word in disgust. "There isn't one other neon sign on Sheridan Road."

It wasn't as if Timber Bay, Michigan, didn't have its share of neon. Ludington Avenue was dotted with it. But the Avenue had always been faster than the Road. Always. The merchants on Sheridan Road tended to keep things just as they always had been. Simple redbrick storefronts marched alongside an old-fashioned theater marquee, a Greek Revival town library and an old wooden band shell that was perched in the park along the bay.

And then there was the Sheridan Hotel. Reclusive town matriarch Agnes Sheridan had hired Danny and Lukas to renovate it. The old lady wanted it restored as closely as possible to its original glory, right down to the intricate wood carvings that Lukas was duplicating to replace sections that had rotted.

Danny slapped him on the back. "A little neon isn't exactly going to ruin the town, pal. Why get all worked up about it?"

It was true that Lukas rarely got all worked up about anything. But this was riling him to no end. "The big-city princess finally claims her inheritance and the first thing she does is plaster neon all over Sheridan Road—and brings in outsiders to do it, besides!"

"They're from Green Bay, Wisconsin, Lukas, not Pluto,"

Danny said as he went around to the back of the truck and let down the gate. "It's sixty miles away."

"Still, what's wrong with hiring somebody local? She's gotta mar the landscape *and* insult the citizens all in one day? And how come you aren't upset, Danny? You're so all-fired excited about preserving stuff. Clemintine's Frocks is nearly as much a fixture on Sheridan Road as the hotel is. We don't need some spoiled city girl coming into town and changing everything around."

"Women have a way of doing that, pal. And it's usually for the better."

Lukas watched the neon being fitted into place and shook his head. "Nothing good is going to come from Gillian Caine coming back to Timber Bay."

GILLIAN SUCKED IN HER TUMMY and eased the side zipper up on her latest creation—a pair of ultraslim cosmic gray satin pants. She sighed with satisfaction. Living on liquid diet shakes for the past week had paid off. She'd lost five of the ten *break-up and go broke* pounds she'd gained back in New York. She lifted the filmy ruffled shirt laid out on the bed and slithered into it. Looking in the full-length mirror in the tiny bedroom of her tiny apartment above Clemintine's Frocks, she was almost satisfied with what she saw.

Of course, it wasn't Clemintine's Frocks any longer, Gillian reminded herself. Along with the five pounds, she'd also shed the wooden sign that had hung over the door for the forty years her Aunt Clemintine had been sole proprietor of the dress shop on Sheridan Road. *Glad Rags.* That's what Gillian's shop was going to be called. In bright, bold pink neon. There were two workmen out front right at that very moment hanging the sign. Which was why Gillian just had to look her very best today. Her most chic. She intended to be as bright an advertisement for Glad Rags as the neon was.

She'd purposely kept a low profile since she'd arrived in Timber Bay less than two weeks ago. Behind the yellowing newspapers that covered the display window, she'd toiled day and night, wallpapering, painting and staining until even the rubber gloves she wore couldn't protect her neglected fingernails. She looked at her hands in disgust.

"Hold on, babies," she cooed to her chipped and ragged nails. "Once we've made our debut, we will find the best manicurist in town and make you all shiny and new again." Nothing wrong that a good nail wrap couldn't cure. But at least the rest of her was looking good.

When she'd arrived in Timber Bay she had still been a mess from the crisis in New York. A girl's world tumbling to pieces around her tended to make for dull hair and muddy-looking skin. So while she'd subsisted on diet shakes, she'd moisturized, exfoliated, mud-packed and conditioned. She leaned in closer to the mirror, scanning her complexion with a critical eye. "Progress," she pronounced with a smile. There were still five pounds to lose but she was looking a whole lot better than when she'd slunk out of NYC on a one-way ticket on Amtrak.

Gillian slipped an ankle-length duster that matched the pants off its hanger and put it on, drawing the deeply ruffled cuffs of the pink georgette shirt out to flounce over her hands. She struggled into the pink crocodile boots filched from what was until only recently her very own—okay, her *co-owned*—boutique in lower Manhattan. They were expensive enough to give Ryan, ex-partner, ex-boyfriend, and ex-decent human being, acid reflux when he realized they were missing. But Gillian had no qualms. In fact, she hoped he'd just downed a double espresso when he discovered the boots were gone and that there wasn't an antacid to be had in all of Manhattan. After what that pseudo-designer and society wannabe had done to her, he was lucky she hadn't taken him to court.

"Enough about him," she said, turning to check out her completed look in the mirror. She smiled hugely at what she saw. There wasn't a woman in Timber Bay under thirty-five who wouldn't be drooling to get inside Glad Rags by the time the grand opening rolled around.

Suddenly her smile faltered, then fell into an outright frown. She had been wrong about Timber Bay in the past. What if—?

Gillian determinedly shook off the thought and the frown. Frowns turned into wrinkles. Besides, she wasn't going to be wrong this time. This time the town was going to want what she had to offer.

They had to. Didn't they? she silently asked her reflection. She'd win them over this time. Wouldn't she?

"Oh, why are you starting with this old insecurity stuff now?" she impatiently asked her reflection. "It is time to *exude* confidence, Gillian! You are no longer a little girl needing acceptance but a businesswoman who will be fulfilling a need in the community." And boy, if they were anything like they used to be, the women of Timber Bay had a really big need for what she had to offer. How could she miss?

Her reflection seemed to be listening to her self-inflicted pep talk. Her shoulders straightened, her chin lifted, and her mouth curved into a smile. "That's more like it." She tucked the large silver clutch bag she'd designed to go with the outfit under her arm and headed down the stairs and out the door.

LUKAS AND DANNY WERE getting ready to unload stacks of lumber for the hotel from the back of the pickup when Danny paused. "Well, look at that," he said under his breath. "A princess from outer space. And I thought Halloween was almost a month away, yet."

Lukas's gaze followed Danny's across the street.

The woman who had just come out the door of the dress shop was wearing something silver. As sleek and shiny as a brand-new saw blade. And she was walking on pink boots with heels as thin and long as a railroad spike. It was some walk she had, too. Lukas knew for sure that there wasn't a woman in town who walked quite that way. She wasn't tall, maybe five foot four, but she had a confident stride for such a shrimp of a girl. And she moved from her hips, causing the fabric of the coat she was wearing to swish back and forth when she walked. Watching her stride over to the workmen was like a compulsion. She said something to them and one of them laughed. For some reason, the sound made Lukas's scowl deepen.

"She still looks like a spoiled big city-princess to me," he muttered.

Danny shrugged. "I guess that must be how they dress in New York City."

"Yeah, but this isn't New York City," Lukas muttered. "No one around here is going to buy that kind of stuff. Now let's get this truck unloaded."

ACROSS THE STREET, Gillian tipped the workmen generously, trying not to calculate how much closer she was going to be to broke because of it. One of the lessons she'd learned from Ryan—besides the need to watch her back—was that you had to look successful to be successful. Money attracted money like lint to black cashmere. Nobody liked to associate with failure. Ryan had always said that looking needy was worse than looking nerdy.

She waved as the workmen drove off, feeling suddenly and absurdly alone. As the truck turned the corner at the Town Square and disappeared down Ludington Avenue, it felt like her last contact with the outside world had been broken. In a way, she supposed, she was like the pioneer women who helped settle the west. Instead of trails forged over mountains or through deserts, she was going to be forging a trail through the closets of Timber Bay, bringing style instead of civilization.

Yes! That was it! A pioneer woman of fashion. She suddenly felt a whole lot better. She also felt hungry—for some real food for a change.

"Time for this pioneer woman to go on a little scouting trip," she murmured to herself as she scanned the street for a sign of someplace to eat. Maybe a nice juicy—

"Mmm, yum," she said under her breath when she looked across the street. Two very juicy guys with a truck. Not exactly what she had in mind, but—

"Oh, swell," she groaned when she got a better look at them.

She hadn't seen either one since they were boys, but she recognized them all the same. Maybe because they were together, just like they'd always been all those summers so long ago. That was Lukas McCoy squatting in the back of the pickup truck. And the other one, the one grinning at her, was Danny Walker. Walker used to tease her mercilessly about wearing the same outfit as the doll she'd always carried around with her. McCoy, who'd been a big, quiet kid, would just sort of scowl at her. Just like he was scowling at her right now.

There had been plenty of kids in Timber Bay who hadn't liked her. But of all of them, McCoy had been the worst. Not that he'd ever said anything. In all the years she'd come to Timber Bay as a child to visit Aunt Clemintine, she'd probably only heard his voice once or twice. But it seemed to her back then that he smiled at everybody else almost all the time. He had these big dimples and they flashed all over the place like the lights in Times Square. Unless, that is, he was looking at her. She seemed to be in some weird no-smile zone as far as he was concerned.

Apparently, from the look on his face, she still dwelled in it.

As a shy little girl her defense had been to stick up her nose and pretend he wasn't there, but she wasn't that girl anymore. Recent events had toughened her up even more. This time, she decided to meet his disapproval head-on. She decided to cross the street.

When she was halfway across, McCoy started to stand up. And up. Gillian's step faltered and slowed as he unfolded and jumped down off the back of the truck.

He was nearly as tall as the dress shop and almost as wide. The scowl hovered on his still boyish face but there was no mistaking the shadow of the dimples on either side of his mouth. With that huge, grown-up body, those blond cherub curls falling over his forehead and that smooth boyish face, a smile would have been enough to make her trip and fall flat on her face. Gillian decided for once that maybe she was glad to be in the no-smile zone.

It occurred to her that she still had time to sort of swerve in her crossing and avoid his orbit altogether, but what the heck. If she could take on Manhattan, she could take on this block of disapproval, as well.

Briefly the thought intruded that she'd lost miserably at taking on Manhattan, but she squashed it down again with the ring of her spiked heel on the cracked pavement of Sheridan Road. She hadn't lost anything—she'd been robbed. Manhattan had been stolen from her, along with her share of the boutique, by her conniving ex and a boney-bottomed lingerie model turned scanty-panty designer. But this small-town giant didn't know that—and neither did anyone else in Timber Bay. And as long as she dripped confidence, style and flare, they never would.

As she neared the other side of the street, Gillian decided it wouldn't hurt to take advantage of the three extra inches the curb offered by stepping onto it. She might as well have dug herself a hole to stand in for all the good those three inches did her. Not to worry, she was used to making up for her shortcomings with bravado.

"I see you've still got your sidekick with you, huh, McCoy?" she asked, with a cocky New-York-City-girl tilt of the head as she looked up at him.

The giant just scowled down at her.

"I don't get kicked that often anymore, though," the other one, Danny Walker, said as he held out his hand. "Welcome back to Timber Bay."

"Well, it's nice to know that one of you has learned some manners, at least," she said, taking his hand.

"Some of us grew up okay," Danny said.

"And some of you just grew, I see."

Lukas knew he was coming across as an oaf. He knew he should be smiling at the lady and making nice. After all, hadn't he just been going on to Danny about "goodwill"? But the big-city princess had always managed to tie his tongue just by looking at him when he was a kid and it looked like nothing much had changed in that department.

As a boy, he used to think she looked like she belonged on top of a fancy birthday cake. She was always dressed in something as light, fluffy and sweet as frosting. She'd been so small with a mass of ash-colored hair hanging down her back and a pair of eyes that looked like they were seeing the world a whole lot differently than anybody else saw it. She still had those eyes. Big. Pale gray irises with dark rings around them. Like the eyes on greeting-card kittens. He'd gone tongue-tied the first time she'd fastened them on him. All he could do was stare. She turned out to be no kitten, though, that little girl from the city. The cat had turned out to be a brat. A snooty, spoiled little girl who didn't like to get dirty and never went anywhere without her doll.

A sudden breeze off the bay lifted her hair and blew it

across her face. It was the same ash color he remembered but cut just above her shoulders now, straight and slick as the skeins of silk yarn his mom embroidered with. She whipped it out of her face with a toss of her head and asked, "Can either of you boys point me in the direction of a decent sandwich?"

This was it, thought Lukas. An opening. Sweet Buns, his sister's coffee shop, was right next to the Sheridan Hotel. Who better to give her the scoop on the place? He opened his mouth, but it felt like he'd walked through a dust storm without a bandanna and nothing came out. As the seconds ticked by, Danny kind of cleared his throat as if to nudge Lukas on. When Lukas tried to lick the dryness from his lips he discovered that his tongue had gone missing.

Finally, Danny started to tell Gillian about Sweet Buns himself. And he was doing it entertainingly enough to get a little giggle out of the girl from New York City. Danny never had any trouble being clever with the ladies. Lukas wished he could think of something clever to say but the longer he stood there, stoically silent, the harder it was to say anything at all—never mind clever.

"I'll move these boards," was all he could finally come up with. He cringed at the lameness of it. And maybe that was why, when he grabbed the small stack of one-by-fours, his grip didn't quite close around them and they went clattering to the sidewalk, grazing the toe of one of Gillian Caine's pink, spike-heeled boots in the process.

She squealed and jumped back, then fixed him with those gray eyes while she stuck her nose into the air. "Is that how you welcome all the new girls to town, McCoy, by nearly crippling them and skinning their shoe leather?"

When he said nothing—and how could he with his mouth full of a brand-new load of sand—Danny swooped in to soothe her and make sure she was okay. Lukas knew he should apologize, but if he couldn't get a word out before he had almost buried her feet in lumber, he sure couldn't spit out any words now.

"You sure you're okay?" he heard Danny ask once again.

"I'm fine, thanks. You've been sweet. But your friend here could obviously use some help in that area. Do the town a favor and don't let him volunteer for the welcoming committee," she said before turning in a swirl of glittering silver and heading down Sheridan Road toward Sweet Buns.

The compulsion still with him, Lukas watched her walk away.

GILLIAN MARCHED INTO Sweet Buns and stopped dead.

"I think I've just found civilization." She closed her eyes and took a deep, long breath in through her nostrils. The aroma nearly made her swoon.

The young woman behind the counter laughed. "Sounds like we have a new coffee addict in town."

"If it tastes as good as it smells, you've got yourself a customer for life."

"Regular or decaf?"

"I'm from New York City." Gillian slid onto a stool at the counter. "What do you think?"

The woman laughed again and poured her a cup of regular. Gillian lifted it to her mouth and took a sip. "Mmm. This is heaven. I never dreamed I'd find a cup of coffee this fantastic so far from Manhattan." She took another swallow, then held out her hand. "I'm Gillian Caine, by the way."

"Yes, I know," the woman behind the counter said as she shook Gillian's hand. "You used to visit your aunt. I'm Molly. Molly Jones."

Gillian shook her head. "I'm sorry, but I don't think I remember you."

"Oh, we weren't friends," Molly quickly added.

Gillian rolled her eyes. "Big surprise. I wasn't exactly

the most popular girl to come to town. Hopefully," she added with a nervous little laugh, "that will change, considering I'm reopening my aunt's dress shop."

"Is what you're wearing an example of what you'll be selling?"

"Yes, it is. I designed it myself." Gillian stood up and gave a little twirl. "What do you think?"

"It's incredible. But—"

"Ma-ma!"

"Oops. Sorry. My little girl is paging me. Be right back."

Molly disappeared into the kitchen and Gillian picked up her coffee cup and strolled around the restaurant. The place was kind of cute with its green gingham curtains and tiny oak tables. Quaint. And the coffee was excellent. When she saw that the beans were sold by the pound, she resolved to buy some to take back to the shop. She was going to be up half the night again, working. On nights like this one was going to be, coffee was a girl's best friend.

In fact, she could use another cup right now. After a few minutes of waiting for a refill, Gillian followed the sounds through the kitchen, out the open back door and into a small fenced-in yard. Molly was bending over a little girl with blond curls and the face of a little angel.

"She's gorgeous!" Gillian exclaimed. "What's her name?"

"This is Chloe. Chloe, say hi to Gillian."

Chloe babbled something incoherently adorable. "Oh, she's so sweet!" said Gillian. "How old is she?"

"Fifteen months. Be careful where you walk, it's a little muddy out here from the rain yesterday."

"Oh, I hope you don't mind that I came out here. I could hear the two of you just babbling away and I thought that since I'm going to be practically a neighbor it'd be okay for me to join in on the girl talk."

Molly lifted Chloe out of the playpen. "No, of course I don't mind. I apologize for abandoning you like that.

This is a slow time of day for Sweet Buns. I've got a few high school girls who help out when it's busy. Now that Chloe is walking, she gets a little restless penned up sometimes."

She put her down on the grass. Chloe immediately went toddling off toward the fence at the back of the yard. The child had excellent taste, Gillian thought. Beyond the fence and across a small sand beach, the bay glittered in the late September sun like the two-carat tanzanite Gillian had seen in the window at Tiffany's.

"It's beautiful out here," Gillian said. "You should offer al fresco dining."

"Someday, maybe," Molly said. "When Chloe's older and I have more time to devote to the business."

Gillian had a million questions to ask about how business was and what the peak hours were at the department store down the street, but the sound of Chloe squealing in delight grabbed her attention. The little girl was toddling with rather alarming speed toward her, gurgling happily about something and waving her little fists up and down.

"She's absolutely, seriously adorable," Gillian gushed, truthfully. Not that Gillian wasn't capable of gushing untruthfully if it might be good for business. But she really did think Chloe was cute.

As Chloe tottered closer, Gillian squatted down and held out her arms to welcome the little cherub. "Come on, Chloe," she cooed. "Come to—"

Chloe squealed, drew back her fisted hands, and let them fly. It turned out that Chloe's little fists hadn't been empty.

Splat!

Gillian's mouth dropped open as mud spattered all over her trousers.

"Chloe!" Molly yelled. "Oh, my gosh! I can't believe she did that! I'm so sorry!"

Chloe giggled and ran back for more mud.

Before she could reach the puddle again, Molly scooped her up and deposited her back into the playpen.

"Gosh! I can't tell you how sorry I am, Gillian. Is it washable?"

Gillian looked at Molly like she'd just spoken a foreign language. "Washable? Of course it's not washable!"

"Oh. Well, then, I'll pay for the dry cleaning. I'm just so sorry."

Gillian could see that Molly really was upset, and besides, Chloe *was* seriously adorable. And it wasn't like Molly had actually invited her into the backyard. Gillian was really sort of trespassing. "Don't worry about it, Molly," she finally said. "It's not your fault. I'm like a walking disaster area today. This is my second accident. See that scuff on my boot? This big blond giant working at the hotel dropped a load of lumber on me."

"Um—blond giant?" Molly asked.

Something about the way Molly sounded made Gillian look at her. That's when she noticed the resemblance. Molly was tall and large-boned with blond hair and warm brown eyes.

"Don't tell me—Lukas McCoy is your brother."

Molly nodded. "Jones is my married name. Gosh, now I feel even worse. The McCoy family hasn't exactly given you a warm welcome, have they?"

"Don't be silly. You've been great. Your brother, however. Well—he was a bit churlish."

"Lukas? Wow, that's not like him."

Gillian already knew that but she saw no point in trying to explain the no-smile zone to Molly.

"Now that I know Lukas ruined your boot, you really have to let me pay for the suit."

"Don't be silly. When the mud dries, it'll probably brush right off."

Molly bit her bottom lip. "You really think so?"

Gillian grimaced. "Uh—no. Probably not. But I don't want you to feel bad about it, okay? Really."

"Well, let's get you something to eat on the house, at least."

She followed Molly inside and sat on a stool at the counter while Molly made her the most delicious chicken salad sandwich she'd ever tasted.

"Why is this so fabulous?" she asked as she took another bite.

"It's the apricot chutney," Molly answered.

"This sandwich almost makes it worth the mud pie appetizer."

Molly laughed. "I'm glad you think so. But wait until you have a sweet bun."

"Oh—no. I couldn't."

"Sure you can! I'll get you another cup of coffee, too."

Despite her protests, when Molly set the frosted cinnamon bun in front of her, Gillian just had to taste it.

As soon as she took the first bite, she knew that a scuffed boot and a mud-spattered suit weren't her only problems. Losing the next five pounds was going to be next to impossible—unless she stayed away from Sweet Buns.

"I'M TELLING YOU, Mother, it's like the McCoy clan has set out to destroy me. This morning that big lug Lukas McCoy nearly dropped a truckload of lumber on my feet. He absolutely ruined those crocodile boots. Then his niece, who is seriously adorable I might add, threw mud all over one of my best designs. And then his sister, Molly, introduces me to the most incredible cinnamon buns I have ever tasted." Gillian paused to swipe her finger over the frosting on the bun Molly had insisted on sending home with her along with a pound of coffee. With the best intentions, she was planning on saving the bun for breakfast. The temptation was killing her.

On the other end of the phone line, her mother laughed.

"Don't be so dramatic, Gilly. That last one doesn't exactly sound like an act of destruction."

Gillian finished licking the frosting off her finger before answering, "That last one could prove very destructive to my waistline."

"You worry too much about your weight, Gilly."

Gillian sighed and swirled her finger into the frosting again. She had long resigned herself to the fact that her girlhood dream of being a model would never come true. She was too short—by model standards, anyway. Five foot four. And both her bottom and her top were far too curvy to ever strut her stuff on the runway. But she had certain standards to maintain. "When you're a housewife in New Jersey, Mother, a couple of pounds isn't going to make a difference. Like the PTA is going to care? But in the fashion industry—"

"In the fashion industry there should be someone who designs for women with fannies and breasts, Gilly. I bet there are a lot of women with fannies and breasts in Timber Bay who would be willing to buy—"

"Mother, if you say *cute little housedresses or caftans* I swear I will scream."

Bonnie Caine laughed. "I doubt even the women in Timber Bay still wear housedresses, Gilly. I just think that instead of starving yourself so you can wear what you design, you should design stuff for women who eat more than fruit and carrot sticks."

Gillian looked longingly at the cinnamon bun as her finger hovered above what was left of its thick white frosting. If this kept up, the poor thing was going to be naked come morning.

"Mother, my mission is to influence the fashion sense of women who think Chanel is something you get on your television set. How can I possibly do that if I become one of them?"

"My darling daughter," her mother said in a dryly amused tone, "I don't think there is any danger of that ever happening."

Gillian decided not to rise to the bait of her mother's teasing. "How's Binky?" she asked instead.

Her mother filled her in on the health and welfare of Binky, the family's twelve-year-old golden retriever, and then on her brothers—all four of them. Then her father butted in on the basement extension and told her, yet again, how he was glad that Ryan was finally out of her life but how he still wished she would have dragged that SOB into court and taken him for everything he had. After he filled her in on the latest skirmish at the boilermakers' union, everyone said goodbye.

As soon as Gillian hung up the phone she felt a stab of homesickness. Yet when she'd gone back to the little blue-collar New Jersey town where she'd grown up after being jilted and swindled, she'd felt less like she belonged there than ever before. She no longer belonged in Manhattan, either. But Timber Bay?

She wandered over to the window in Aunt Clemintine's living room and looked down onto Sheridan Road. It was late afternoon and the setting sun had streaked the clouds with pink and gold. The Road was bustling with people heading home for the day. Across the street at Sweet Buns, Molly was turning the sign hanging in the door around to read *Closed*—probably getting ready to go upstairs with little Chloe for the evening.

"Chloe," Gillian groaned out loud. Mud pies! Served all over the outfit that was supposed to be the centerpiece of her *Pastel-Metallic* collection. The duster was salvageable. But the pants were a mess. Which meant that Gillian had better get back to work.

As soon as she ran down the stairs and through the door that led to the workroom behind the shop, she felt at home. As much of a misfit as she'd been as a kid, she'd always felt completely comfortable in the back room of her aunt's dress shop. Aunt Clemintine had taught her all she knew about garment construction. They'd spent wonderful, happy hours together, making clothes for Gillian and her doll. Her family was blue collar and money hadn't exactly been growing on trees, but Gillian, thanks to Aunt Clemintine, had dressed like a million bucks.

But it wasn't only the clothes, it was the attention that made her love to visit Aunt Clemintine so much. Back at home, she was the middle child, crowded on both sides by two younger and two older brothers. So around their house it was jock central. Her parents were loving and wonderful, but a little girl who didn't like sports pretty much got overlooked and out-voiced. Aunt Clemintine, a childless spinster, gave Gillian a place to be safe while she discovered who she was and what she wanted to be. And what she wanted to be was as different as she could possibly be from anything like home.

Unfortunately, as Gillian grew older, Aunt Clemintine and the dress shop got lumped in with everything that Gillian wanted to leave behind. When Aunt Clemintine had died a few years ago and left Gillian the shop, Gillian was touched. But she could just never see herself claiming her inheritance and taking up residence in Timber Bay.

Now she didn't know how she could have stayed away as long as she had.

The workroom welcomed her warmly, just as it always did. The little puffy calico pincushions scattered about the workspaces. The smell of new cloth, not yet handled or wrinkled. She ran her hand over a bolt of ivory silk and closed her eyes at the feel of it. By the time she opened them, she was smiling again.

The workroom was exactly where she needed to be right now. And not just because she still had clothing to finish before the opening, but because hitting the streets of Timber Bay for the first time hadn't turned out as she'd hoped and talking to her mother and father had left her a little lonely.

"Come here, you gorgeous piece of goods, you," she purred to the bolt of silk as she picked it up. "I think tonight is your night to become Cinderella."

Several hours later, the ivory silk was sliding over her head and floating down her body. Gillian ran out to the dark shop, switched on the light, then closed her eyes as she made her way to the triple mirror near the dressing room, her arms out straight, palms extended. She'd played this scene over and over again as a little girl. She used to be able to find that mirror walking blind. Her outstretched palms hit the cool glass and she smiled. She'd gone right to it.

When she opened her eyes, she was still smiling. The dress looked spectacular. The front neckline draped low enough to show just a hint of décolletage. The back dipped even lower—nearly to her waist—and ended in a flirty bow. The bodice was fitted and the calf-length skirt was full and fluttery. Grace Kelly meets the twenty-first century. Exactly the effect she had been going for.

Gillian stood on tiptoes to try to envision how the skirt would fall if she was wearing high heels, then remembered that she'd brought down a pair of silver strappy sandals the night before. She scampered around the shop till she found them in a corner, then went back to the mirror.

Perfect.

"You are going to look so terrific in the window," she told the dress. "With that vintage faux pearl jewelry. And maybe a soft pink wool stole to go with the neon sign. Or a cloak. Pink cashmere."

She pursed her lips wryly and shook her head at her reflection. Talk about dreaming big.

"Well, pink something," she told herself, refusing to let

the price of cashmere ruin the moment. Pink like the Glad Rags logo and sign.

And that reminded her. She hadn't yet seen the new sign after dark. Gillian threaded her way through unpacked cartons, naked mannequins and hatless hat stands, to the front door. She unlocked it and went outside.

There it was, glowing across the display window in lovely pink neon. Glad Rags. The sight of it put a huge grin on her face and made her twirl around in delight. Quickly, she looked around to make sure there were no witnesses to her less-than-sophisticated display of girlish goofiness.

Not a soul in sight. Different from Manhattan as silk from corduroy. Yet she felt hopeful for the first time in months. Gillian was nearly giddy as she ran across the street to see what the sign looked like from farther away. Maybe it was the air. It was crisp and pure with a tang of water in the wind. The hotel blocked the bay from sight, but she could still hear the waves faintly. Still feel the presence of it on her skin. She started back across the street but paused midway to look up at the sky. So many stars. Even when she was a kid in New Jersey, there hadn't been so many stars in the sky. She picked out the brightest one and closed her eyes.

"I wish," she whispered....

That's when she heard the noise—quickly followed by the feel of the ground beneath her feet shifting jerkily.

And the next thing she knew, she was flying through the air.

She put out her arm to break her fall and felt the jar of the impact all the way up to her shoulder. She grimaced as her palm scraped against the concrete. For a minute, everything went out of focus and then her sight cleared and she saw the dark bulk of a man emerging from the concrete.

"I promised to make you a Cinderella," she murmured to the silk that seemed to have turned into a cloud around her. "But that doesn't look at all like Prince Charming."

He looked more like some sort of beast who made his home in the bowels of the earth. He kept rising and rising and rising, and it was making Gillian dizzy as hell to have to look up so high. Or was it the pain that suddenly shot through her arm when she tried to move? Either way, Gillian did something she'd never done before.

She fainted.

2

ABOVE THE NOISE of the manhole cover clattering to the street, Lukas heard another sound. High-pitched. Like a woman's squeal.

"Did you hear that?" he asked the big orange tabby cat that was tucked under his arm. The cat flattened its ears and growled. Lukas let go of it and it shot off into the darkness. He hoisted himself out of the manhole and looked around.

The night was clear and crisp, the sky thick with stars. He turned slowly around, trying to remember what he'd learned as a kid about astronomy. All he remembered was that nothing looked like it was supposed to. The names made no sense to him at all. Except maybe the Big Dipper. He could always find that. Tonight it seemed full of stardust.

"You're getting fanciful, Lukas. You better watch that," he muttered to himself as he dragged the manhole cover back into place. He straightened up and that's when he saw it. Something lying in the street. Something as bright and shimmery as a heap of stardust fallen from the sky.

When the heap of stardust moaned and shifted slightly Lukas went closer and found himself looking down at the body of Gillian Caine.

He sucked in his breath, then hunkered down next to her. "Gillian," he said softly, touching her on the shoulder. She didn't move. He found the pulse in her neck with his fingers. Oh man, was she soft. And her heart felt like it was beating pretty good, too. She moaned again and he snatched his fingers back. Her eyes stayed closed so he touched her hair for no good reason at all except that, there, just outside of the circle of light from a street lamp, it looked like it was shot with silver. She moaned again and her lashes fluttered.

"Gillian?" he repeated.

She smiled a little this time. A small, sweet smile. In fact, the princess looked altogether sweeter when she was passed out cold than she had when he'd seen her that afternoon.

She was wearing a pale dress made of something silky. It floated around her, settling in the swells and hollows of her body, and fluttered out around the curves of her calves. Her shoes were worthy of a princess, too. Glittery silver with tiny straps and skinny heels that were made out of something as transparent as glass.

"Gillian?" Still no response. He frowned. Shouldn't she be coming to by now? He looked around the street. All the buildings were dark. Even the windows above Sweet Buns where his sister lived were dark. Molly must have already gone to bed. Timber Bay Memorial was only a mile or so down Ludington Avenue. Lukas figured he could get Gillian to the hospital himself in less time than it would take him to rouse Molly, use her phone, then wait for an ambulance to come.

Carefully he started to gather Gillian up in his arms. She felt so small. A wounded helpless creature. As he started to lift her, his nose brushed her neck. The scent of her shot through him like a craving. The urge was strong to bury his face in the soft crook of her neck. Just for a moment, he told himself.

"Who are you and why are you sniffing my neck?"

Lukas pulled his head back quick enough to give himself whiplash. He knew his face must be flaming.

"Lukas McCoy," Gillian mumbled fuzzily. "I should

have known." She looked around, still obviously in a daze. "What am I doing in the middle of the road?"

Before he could answer, she started to get up and moaned loudly.

"Ohh—my arm. What happened?"

"Near as I can tell, you must have been standing on that manhole cover over there when I—"

Gillian gasped. "Now I remember! You were that beast who came up out of the concrete and sent me sailing into the air, aren't you? What is it with you McCoys, anyway?"

"What does that mean?"

She shook her head. "Oh, never mind. Just help me up."

Lukas helped her struggle to her feet.

"What were you doing, anyway?" she asked. "Lying in wait, hoping to get a second chance after your earlier attempt at crippling me failed?"

"Hey—that was an accident," Lukas said a little bluntly—more bluntly than he should have. The bright idea of Gillian Caine being wounded and helpless was definitely losing its shine.

"Tell that to the thousand-dollar pair of boots you ruined. And I suppose this was an accident, too. Just you crawling out of the sewer after a day of Dungeons and Dragons?"

"I was down in the tunnel of love to—"

Gillian shot him a sharp look with those huge gray eyes. "The tunnel of *what*?" she asked him, scrunching up her nose. "Did you say the *tunnel of love*?"

Lukas hadn't meant to say that. He felt foolish enough for knocking her flying and the knowledge that he'd wrecked a thousand bucks' worth of leather wasn't sitting too well, either. He didn't relish the idea of trying to explain the legend of Timber Bay's tunnel of love to the princess when she was acting more like the wicked queen. "Look, maybe we better see about getting you to a doctor," he said as he took her gently by the other arm.

"I don't need a doctor," she said, pulling away from him and jostling her wounded arm in the process. "Ow!" She grimaced. "Okay, maybe I do need a doctor."

"My truck is right across the street. I'll take you."

Lukas didn't know much about body language, but Gillian made it clear she didn't want his help getting across the street. It was kind of amazing, really, he thought as he followed her to the truck, that she could walk like she did on a pair of heels like that after she'd just been out cold. She made it look as if balancing on three inches of acrylic was the most natural thing in the world.

He opened the door for her and tried to help her in, bumping her shoulder in the process.

"Ow!" she said again, as she shot an angry wounded look at him with those big gray eyes.

"Sorry," he said as he dipped his head. "I guess I can be kind of a bull in a drugstore."

"China shop," she said.

"Huh?"

"Bull in a china shop. You said drugstore."

"Oh—that's because when I was twelve I was kind of big for my age and there was this sort of pyramid of perfume bottles stacked up on the counter at Ludington Drugs and one day I went charging right into them, breaking every last one. The whole town square smelled like lavender water for a week. Ever since then—" He gulped, wishing he'd stayed tongue-tied. She was looking at him like he'd gone around the bend. Which he must have because here he was standing in front of the most beautiful woman he'd ever seen and rattling on about his damn clumsiness after he'd just given her a demonstration of it by busting up her arm.

"Look," she said. "I'm sure this folksy charm works on all the local girls, but I've got the disadvantage here of being in pain. Let's save your life story for after I'm medicated, okay?"

Lukas clamped his mouth shut and managed to help her up into the truck and shut the door without jostling her again. When he went around to the other side and got in, the cab was already full of the scent of her skin. It tied his tongue up all over again. Good thing, too. Otherwise, the big-city princess might have managed to bite it the rest of the way off.

GILLIAN FUMED as the truck turned onto Ludington Avenue. Her arm was killing her and the big lug wasn't even going to bother saying he was sorry. She looked at him out of the corner of her eye. Make that big adorable lug. That tousled hair the color of pale honey that fell over his forehead in loose curls. That snub nose and small, sensual mouth. On another man it all might have looked wimpy. But on top of that big body, it just made him look like a small-town Tarzan. No—make that lumberjack. He worked with wood. She knew that much. She could smell it on him and there was sawdust on the plaid shirt he wore tucked into jeans that hugged his massive thighs and made his—

Gillian blinked. What in the name of *Vogue* magazine was she thinking? Well, she was thinking about what big, hard-looking thighs he had and about what they might feel like if she just reached out and...

This time she blinked and bit her lip at the same time. She deliberately jarred her arm just so she could feel the pain and remember that she had no business whatsoever ogling Paul Bunyan's thighs.

"Are you all right?" he asked when she gasped in pain.

"No, I am not all right. Thanks to you," she added testily, reminding herself that he still hadn't said he was sorry for what he'd done. "I just hope you've got your checkbook with you."

He glanced her way. "My checkbook?"

"This," she indicated her arm, "is all your fault and you're paying for the emergency room."

"Of course I'll pay. And I'll give you the money for those overpriced boots, too. But no way am I taking the complete blame this time."

"Um—reality check. You *are* completely to blame."

"You were the one standing out in the middle of the street. They teach you to do that out there in New York City? Cause we don't teach kids in Timber Bay to stand out in the street much."

"It's the middle of the night. Who knew it wouldn't be safe to cross the street?"

"You weren't crossing, you were standing."

"I mean—" she went on as if he hadn't spoken "—who knew that a giant prowled under the streets of Timber Bay at night and that there was always the danger of him just breaking through the damn concrete whenever he felt like it—no matter who was standing there?"

As far as Lukas was concerned, she was being totally unreasonable. "You were standing on a manhole. I'm a man. You gotta expect these things sometimes."

"That is totally insane. I was safer in the streets of New York than I am here. First you throw a pile of wood at me—"

"That was an accident!"

"Then your niece ruins a few hundred dollars' worth of cosmic gray metallic satin—"

"Chloe? Chloe ruined that silver thing you were wearing?"

"Cosmic gray," she repeated through clenched jaws. "And yes. She ruined it when she decided to serve me mud pies."

"Hey, Chloe is a sweet kid but she's not even a year-and-a-half old yet."

"So what's your excuse?"

"Listen, princess, I said I was sorry—"

"What did you call me?"

"Princess."

"Don't call me that."

"Ha. Did I strike a nerve, princess?"

"I told you not to call me that. And no, you did not."

"No, I did not what?"

"You did not say you were sorry. Not even once."

Hadn't he? Lukas ran over the past minutes in his mind. He must have said he was sorry. But as he pulled into the hospital parking lot and drove around back to the emergency entrance, he honestly could not remember apologizing.

He parked, got out of the truck, and went around to the passenger side to open the door for Gillian. He helped her out as carefully as possible. He could see it cost her some to let him. He had the feeling that at this point she'd rather kick him in the shins with her silver slipper than take his arm.

As soon as the electronic doors swooshed open and let them inside the hospital, Gillian was swept away. He paced while he waited for her to fill out forms and answer questions. He thought he'd get to talk to her when she was sent to the waiting area, but she'd no sooner sat down than a nurse came out and got her. Slow night, apparently, in the E.R. Lukas had never wished for other people to have bad fortune in order that he might get something he wanted, but he sure could have used a little laceration, or a broken toe maybe, so he'd have enough time to apologize to Gillian. Because she'd been right about that, at least. He hadn't apologized.

What was the matter with him? Lukas never, ever argued with women. Oh, he and his sister Molly tussled like all brothers and sisters, but as far as other women went, Lukas was pretty easygoing. So what had gotten into him tonight? Gillian could have a broken arm and it was all because of him. He remembered how her face had grimaced in pain, and felt ashamed for arguing with her when she was hurt. His mom would skin him alive if she knew.

As he always did when he was bothered by something, Lukas pulled out the piece of wood he kept in one pocket and the knife he kept in the other and sat down in the waiting room to whittle. He knew from the night Chloe was born that the hospital staff wasn't crazy about having shavings all over the waiting-room floor so he mostly just worked on smoothing out the lines of the chess piece he was carving. When he heard the click of high heels on tile, he looked up to see Gillian coming down the short corridor between the treatment cubicles and the waiting room. Her left arm was in a sling. Oh, man. His heart swelled when he saw it. It must be serious. And it was his fault. And he hadn't even said he was sorry.

He got up and started toward her. "I—" he began.

"You," she said, sticking out her good arm, palm up like a traffic cop, "don't come one step closer."

She sailed past him and was nearly to the exit doors before he got his wits about him.

"Wait! What did the doctor say?"

She turned around. "It's *sprained*, McCoy, that's what he says. My arm is sprained. I have to keep it in this—this sling. And he says it'll be a couple of weeks before I can fully use it again. A couple of weeks, McCoy. I don't have a couple of weeks. I've got a boutique to get ready to open. Now how do you suppose I'm going to be able to do that with only one arm?"

She started for the door again. He couldn't let her get away without apologizing.

"But—wait! I'll drive you home. I want to—"

"I called a cab. There is no way I'm getting that close to

you—or any other member of your family—ever again," she called over her shoulder just as the doors slid closed.

Lukas ran to catch up to her, but by the time the doors opened again and he hurried outside, the cab was already pulling away.

"Ow!" Gillian exclaimed when she stuck herself in the hand with a seam ripper for the fourth time. "This is impossible," she grumbled, throwing down the cosmic gray satin pants. She'd been hoping that she could salvage the pants because there was just enough of the fabric left to replace the front where Chloe had served her the mud pies, but with one arm in a sling, the seams had ended up looking like the sewing machine needle was going for Olympic gold in the slalom race. She'd assumed that it would be easier to rip out a seam than sew one. But despite the fact that she was right-handed and it was her left arm in the sling, it was still remarkably hard to do anything one-handed.

Gillian finally gave up on the pants and started to unpack the ready-to-wear lingerie she'd ordered. Some of the items needed steaming. She was able to do this pretty well with one hand, but it did nothing to lighten her mood. The silky slips, the gossamer gowns and robes, the lacy bra and panty sets, just made her more aware of the fact that there was going to be more lingerie in the shop than there was going to be Glad Rags by Gillian. She could have wept with frustration. Glad Rags was supposed to showcase her own designs, not those of already established lingerie designers who didn't even need the measly sales they'd get in Timber Bay, anyway.

After what Ryan had done to her, Gillian had only been able to put one foot in front of the other by chanting *living well is the best revenge* like a mantra every time the blues threatened. For weeks she'd sustained herself on the image of women flocking to the door of Glad Rags as soon as she unlocked it on the opening day of the Harvest Festival and Sale. She had even done the heretofore unheard-of and toned down her styles for Midwestern tastes. But that hadn't been sacrifice enough to appease the gods of failure because now her dreams of success—her meager dreams of revenge—were disappearing faster than tickets to a hit Broadway musical. And all because of Lukas McCoy.

A stream of too-hot mist hissed out of the steamer, nearly hot enough to melt the fine lace edging on the camisole she was working on. "Easy, Gilly," she said, "it's Lukas McCoy you want to melt, not this exquisite lace."

Abruptly, she stopped moving the steamer up and down. Had she said *melt*? Nonsense. Gillian started steaming again. Stopped again. *Had* she? Well, if she had, she told herself, what she'd meant to say was fry. No, that was the electric chair. Burn? Hmm. Well, certainly not melt. Melting implied all sorts of gooey feelings. And she wasn't feeling gooey at all towards McCoy. She had no intention of getting all gooey over any man ever again.

Nor did she have any intention of steaming one more garment that she hadn't designed herself.

Not today, anyway.

Gillian went upstairs to Aunt Clemintine's apartment to make a pot of coffee. As soon as the aroma drifted up from the coffeemaker, she wished she had one of Molly's cinnamon buns. Sweet Buns was just across the street. She could hop over there, get a bun, and come back before the coffee was even done brewing. But Molly was a McCoy. And it wasn't safe for her to go near a McCoy.

She took a cup of coffee into the living room and prepared to chill out by doing some channel surfing. Aunt Clemintine's taste had run to overstuffed chintz, Italian porcelain flower arrangements, and numerous other girly bric-a-brac that Gillian had loved when she was a little girl. It was so feminine compared to her parents' house which had been overrun with boy stuff and decorated chiefly with anything that wouldn't break easily or show dirt.

Gillian opened the doors to the antique armoire that contained a little television set, then got comfortable on the overstuffed sofa. But when she reached for the remote control, it wasn't on the coffee table. Or the end table. It wasn't anywhere. It took her five minutes of searching before she realized that the only innovation Aunt Clemintine had embraced after 1952 had been polyester fabric. Her TV didn't have a remote. It didn't even have color. Gillian ended up sitting crossed-legged on the floor close enough to the set to reach out and change the channels manually.

The soaps were no fun in black-and-white because you couldn't really enjoy the clothes. She stopped at a courtroom show—one of those half-hour things where a smart-aleck judge badgered and humiliated the stuffing out of either the defendant or the plaintiff—or sometimes both. Not Gillian's idea of happy viewing. She reached out to change the channel when something the female plaintiff said caught her attention.

"It's his fault, Your Honor, how was I supposed to deliver pizzas after he wrecked my car? I got no earnings—he should be made to pay."

The judge, a feisty-looking middle-aged woman, asked some questions, listened to the answers, and then lashed into the male defendant like her tongue was a cat-o-nine-tails. The defendant tried to defend himself. The judge shut him up. By the time she threw the book at him and made him pay damages and lost wages, Gillian was up on her feet cheering.

"Damn, that felt good," she said, nearly out of breath with *sisters unite* blood lust. And then it hit her.

Maybe she should sue Lukas McCoy.

She started to pace the small living room.

Could she?

Should she?

Would she?

Gillian could feel her adrenaline pumping at the thought of having her day in court. Oh, she really wasn't out for blood. She didn't want to ruin McCoy or anything. She just wanted enough money to be able to afford to hire someone to be her left arm until it healed. She'd been too big a wimp to do anything about what Ryan had done to her. But that didn't mean she had to go on being a wimp, did it? She didn't want to continue allowing men to screw up her life and livelihood, did it?

"Absolutely not!"

She marched over to Aunt Clemintine's little phone stand and picked up the Timber Bay phone book. "I've got more numbers than this in my Rolodex," she muttered as she flipped through the slim volume until she found the yellow pages. All eight of them. She located the listing for lawyers and picked up the phone.

LUKAS WAS SITTING on the railing that surrounded the marble terrace at the back of the Sheridan Hotel. It was one of those perfect late September days when the leaves on the trees had started to turn but hadn't yet started to fall. They rustled in the wind off the bay—a last gasp of energy before the colder winds of October put them to rest on the ground. Climbing roses that had been allowed to go wild were still blooming and there were clusters of deep-gold mums, some of them almost as big as shrubs, bordering the low wall that ran down to the water. He could hear the rhythmic lap of the waves against the ramshackle pier.

If things went the way Agnes Sheridan wanted them to, by next summer the small pier would be restored and there'd be boats docked there. The roses would be tamed and there would be people sitting on the terrace. Wealthy, worldly people.

People like Gillian Caine.

"If only I'd said I was sorry," he mumbled.

"What's that, pal?"

Lukas started at the sound of Danny's voice, then quickly collected himself. "About time you got back with my lunch," Lukas said, figuring a little grousing would make Danny forget that Lukas hadn't answered him.

"Here ya go." Danny tossed Lukas a bag from the lunch counter at Ludington Drugs. "Tuna salad on white bread and an order of fried chicken. Interesting combination."

Lukas easily caught the bag. He rummaged inside and came out with the sandwich. "Did you tell Clara to put cheese on the tuna?"

"Yup."

Lukas unwrapped the sandwich and started to tear it into little pieces.

Danny groaned. "Don't tell me you found another stray?"

Lukas set the wrapper down at the top of the steps and called, "Here, Tiger, Tiger."

A huge clump of mums started to rustle. A moment later a cat emerged—the same one he'd rescued from the tunnel. The big, lazy-moving orange tabby had a scar on his nose and half his tail was missing. He prowled over to sniff the sandwich, gave Lukas a look of appreciation, then delicately started to eat.

Danny laughed. "Cat knows a good thing. Clara uses only albacore down at Ludington's. By the time you get around to buying cat food, that cat is gonna turn up his nose at it."

"You can tell just by looking at him that he's been through a lot. He's got a little luxury coming," Lukas said as he bit into a chicken leg.

"Next thing you know, you'll be going over to Sweet Buns and getting him a slice of cheesecake."

Lukas laughed. What Danny said wasn't so far-fetched. Lukas had been rescuing things all his life. As recently as last month he'd coaxed a wounded squirrel with macadamia nuts filched from the larder at Sweet Buns that, Molly never stopped reminding him, weren't exactly cheap. He regularly climbed trees to fetch cats and helped old ladies cross the street. Heck, he'd even rescued Danny from a bunch of bullies back in grade school. They'd been best buddies ever since. Lukas had a reputation of being an all-around good guy. So how come he'd acted the way he had with Gillian Caine?

"You know, buddy, I did a really stupid thing the other night," Lukas said to Danny.

"Stupider than feeding a stray cat a three-dollar sandwich?"

"Afraid so. I was down in the hotel's wine cellar measuring for the new fittings, when I thought I heard a cat yowling in the tunnel. I checked it out and, sure enough, Tiger here was trapped down there. He was kind of spooked—clawing the hell out of me—and I remembered how when you and Hannah were trapped down there you got out through a manhole onto Sheridan Road. So Tiger and I took the same shortcut."

Danny shrugged. "What's so stupid about that? Don't tell me you had trouble pushing that cover aside. If Hannah could do it—"

"Oh, I could push it out of the way all right, no problem. Trouble is, I sort of pushed more than the manhole cover out of the way."

Danny wrinkled his brow. "What else did you push?"

"Gillian Caine. She was standing on the cover and she sort of went airborne."

Danny started to laugh.

"It's not funny, Danny. She sprained her arm. I had to

take her to the E.R. and she's got to wear a sling and I didn't even say I was sorry."

"Well, that's not like you, pal. You're the polite type. You even manage to be nice to Dragon Lady Sheridan."

"Danny, I gotta tell you, I feel really lousy about this. She looked so little and helpless laying there in the street—"

"Gillian Caine helpless?"

"Maybe I should send her some flowers or something. What do you think?" Lukas asked earnestly.

Before Danny could answer, Tiger gave a growl worthy of a canine and both Danny and Lukas turned to see what he was tracking with his yellow stare. A man in a suit was standing in the open French doors.

"Which one of you is Lukas McCoy?"

Tiger bolted back into the mums as Lukas wiped his fingers on a paper napkin and stood up. "I'm McCoy," he said.

"Then this is for you." The man handed Lukas some papers and rapidly retreated.

"Hey, wait!" Lukas called to his back, but the guy just kept going.

"What's with the papers?" Danny asked.

Lukas looked down at them. It took him a few moments to comprehend what he was reading. "Unbelieeeeevable!" He thrust a hand into his hair and started to pace the terrace while he read it again just to be sure. "Un-damn-believable."

"What is it?" Danny asked.

Lukas looked up. "Gillian Caine is suing me."

Danny whistled, long and low. "I guess it's a good thing you didn't order those flowers yet, huh, pal?"

"I do hope," said a familiar voice from just inside the French doors, "that this doesn't mean that my grandson was right about the two of you."

"Mrs. Sheridan," Lukas said with surprise. "Did we have an appointment? How long have you—um—"

"Been standing here?" the old lady finished for him.

"Long enough to know that someone is suing you. Long enough to make me wonder if I've made a mistake."

Danny hopped to his feet. "You know nothing about what's going on, so if I were you—"

Lukas stepped in front of Danny, cutting him off both literally and figuratively. "What you just heard, Mrs. Sheridan, had nothing to do with Timber Bay Building and Restoration. It's me getting sued. Not the company."

Danny poked his head around Lukas. "Not that it'd be any of Gavin's business either way."

"That's where you're wrong," Agnes Sheridan said with a haughty thrust of her head. "Gavin is coming back to Timber Bay."

Behind him, Danny swore and Lukas tried to cover it up with a cough. "That's—um—swell, Mrs. Sheridan," he said after he'd cleared the imaginary frog in his throat.

The old lady's black eyes glittered and her thin, usually stubbornly set mouth, actually smiled. "It's what I had hoped. That once work started on the hotel, Gavin would take an interest and reclaim his life in Timber Bay."

"Don't tell me he's coming home for good?" Danny asked.

"One can hope, Mr. Walker."

"Yes," Danny agreed. "One can."

Lukas was pretty sure that Danny and Agnes Sheridan weren't hoping the same thing. He'd feel safer if he separated the two of them.

"Mrs. Sheridan, why don't you let me show you the progress I'm making in the lobby. I think you'll be pleased with the way the staircase looks."

"Lead on, young man," she said. But before she went through the French doors she turned and gave Danny a poke in the leg with her cane. "I suggest you get on with your lunch, Walker. I assure you that Gavin won't take this sitting about on the job any better than I do."

Danny opened his mouth but before anything could come

out, Lukas took the Dragon Lady by the arm and ushered her into the ballroom, closing the French doors behind them.

Danny and the Dragon Lady had been enemies for years. Things had gotten better since Hannah, who Agnes Sheridan totally approved of, had hit town. But now that Gavin was coming back, Lukas was going to have his hands full as a peacemaker. The last thing he needed right now was to have some big-city brat take him to court.

He'd been right. Nothing good was coming from Gillian Caine being back in Timber Bay.

"THE HEARING IS TOMORROW, Mom," Gillian said into the phone receiver.

"Justice moves swiftly in the Midwest."

"They've got this judge who takes care of several counties and he's only in town once a month. How primitive is that? My lawyer—who, by the way, I had to go to the next town to get—said that if we didn't get on the docket this time, we'd have to wait a whole month."

"Are you sure you're doing the right thing, Gilly?"

Gillian sighed. "What are you trying to say, Mom?"

"Well, as I remember it, the McCoys were well liked in Timber Bay. The town might not take too kindly to an outsider taking one of their own to court. Have you thought of what it might do to business?"

"Mom, I'm not planning on taking him to the cleaners. I just want enough to hire someone to help me for the next couple of weeks."

"But, honey, I already offered to come out and—"

"Forget it, Mom. We've been through all this already. I need to do this on my own. I need to be totally independent."

"You don't have to prove anything to anyone, Gilly."

Her mother was wrong. Gillian had to prove something to herself. She had to prove that she could be her own person and not have to count on anyone coming through for her ever again. If she failed, she'd have no one to blame but herself. And if she succeeded, no one could ever take it away from her.

"Can't you just be supportive, Mom? I mean, Dad keeps saying that he wishes I hadn't let Ryan off the hook. You should be jumping up and down with joy. I finally think Dad was right about something. I shouldn't have let Ryan get away with it. I'm not making that mistake again."

"But, Gilly, it's not the same thing at all. In fact—"

Gillian was picking at a fingernail and mostly tuning her mother out when she heard a knock on the door downstairs.

"Mom, someone's at the door," she said, sending silent gratitude to whoever it was for getting her out of this conversation. She loved her mother, but she had heard it all before. "I'll call you after court tomorrow. Kisses to everyone," she added as brightly as possible. "Bye!"

She hurried downstairs and through the workroom to the back door. But when she opened it, no one was there. Sitting on the cement stoop was a wicker basket covered with a green-and-white gingham napkin. She recognized the napkin, but even if she hadn't, she would have known that Molly had left the basket. Gillian could smell the cinnamon buns that were lurking beneath the gingham.

A bribe.

She snatched the basket up, shut the door and locked it behind her.

The smart thing would be to leave the basket downstairs in the workroom. Or better yet, out in the shop. Less temptation that way.

On the other hand, it was an old building. It wouldn't do to encourage any rodents that might have designs on the place—make them think they were going to be able to stop in for a midnight snack.

She decided that she better take the basket upstairs with her, after all. That didn't mean she was accepting the bribe, though, she told herself, climbing the stairs. She was a big girl. She could certainly resist a couple of cinnamon buns.

When she put the basket on the small drop-leaf table in the kitchen, she noticed the note tucked inside. With two fingers she carefully pulled it out, trying not to disturb the napkin and have to actually look the bribe in the eye. Or in this case, in the frosting.

I thought you might feel funny about coming into Sweet Buns so sweet buns are coming to you. Sorry again for the mud pies. Molly.

"Mud pies. Huh—yeah, right," Gillian muttered. The basket was an obvious attempt to sweeten her up and make her drop the suit. She wondered how many cinnamon buns Molly thought it would take to buy her.

Well, she could just keep wondering because there was no way she was lifting that napkin and looking underneath.

Stoically, she marched into the bedroom. There were several outfits laid out on the canopy bed Aunt Clemintine had gotten for her the summer she'd turned six. Gillian was still trying to decide what to wear to court the next day.

"Something feminine, yet strong," she murmured.

That left out the pink polka-dot suit with the ruffled hems.

"Something strong, yet sympathetic."

That left out the black shantung tuxedo with the sheer tailored shirt and her witty take on a men's club tie (diagonal rows of pink poodles against an aqua background).

"Something—" Well, above all something that would go with her sling. Which, she supposed, would be the black sleeveless sheath with the little turquoise capelet. The only problem was that it was very, very formfitting. But she *had* just lost five pounds.

When she tried it on, it fit beautifully. She didn't even have to hold her tummy in—much. And it barely hurt her arm to put it on.

"Perfect," she pronounced as she looked in the mirror.

Whoever invented those diet shakes should get the Nobel or something. She had missed chewing, though. The sensual feel of food actually in her mouth. Hmm. And that reminded her. She hadn't had any dinner yet. She'd picked up a salad at the supermarket and it was waiting in the fridge. She peeled out of the dress, hung it up and headed for the kitchen.

Was it her imagination or had the basket from Sweet Buns gotten bigger? Gillian ignored it and went to the fridge. She grabbed the salad, wrestled off the plastic cover and dug in.

"Oh, yum," she muttered with her mouth full. "Iceberg lettuce and hothouse tomatoes."

She kept forking into the salad but her stomach kept right on growling. Or was it the siren song of the cinnamon buns she kept hearing over the crunch of a woody radish?

Gillian eyed the basket. It would be such a shame to waste those buns. And didn't carbohydrates help induce sleep? She started to reach for the basket, then drew her hand back. But, if the buns really were a bribe, did that mean that if she ate one she'd be accepting the bribe?

She picked up the note and read it again.

There really was no mention of Lukas, or the court case, at all. And she was, after all, owed some sort of payment for the pants that adorable Chloe ruined. Just a little carbohydrate to soothe the nerves. It'd be the healthy thing to do, wouldn't it?

She pulled back the napkin. Six large buns, slathered with thick frosting, were nestled oh-so-beautifully in another gingham napkin. It was more than Gillian could stand.

Just one, she thought. One wouldn't hurt.

3

IT WAS NEARLY TIME to leave for court and Gillian was still struggling with the side zipper on the black sheath. It turned out that the cinnamon buns hadn't been a bribe at all. Sabotage. That's what they were. Sabotage to make her gain back those five pounds.

Of course, no one had made her eat all six of them.

"But Molly should have known I couldn't resist!" she wailed at her bloated reflection. Following a half-dozen sweet buns from Sweet Buns, the dress had ceased being a sheath and had turned, overnight, into a sausage.

Gillian gave up on the zipper and started to rip the dress off.

"Ow!"

Drat her sprained arm. It made dressing, something Gillian ordinarily loved to do, nearly impossible and painful as the dentist.

Okay, maybe it wasn't as bad as a root canal. But it was so frustrating to have to do everything not only one-handed but gingerly, as well. She couldn't wait to face Lukas McCoy in court. If the judge didn't throw the book at him, Gillian just might have to throw something at him herself.

One-handed, of course.

She yanked a sleeveless red shirtwaist with a retro full skirt out of the closet and struggled into it, managing to howl in pain only twice. It had a wide belt that was, thankfully, adjustable, and even though it was a little snug in the bodice the full skirt definitely hid any evidence of her carbo pig-out session the night before. She took a white cardigan sweater that she'd picked up in a vintage clothing shop in the Village out of Aunt Clemintine's bureau. It had a darling little Peter Pan collar that was edged with tiny seed pearls. Perfect for throwing over her shoulders. She slipped red pumps on her bare feet—panty hose had proven impossible to maneuver with only one hand— transferred the necessary junk to a vintage red clutch purse, then checked herself in the mirror.

"Hmm, not bad," she murmured. Maybe even better than the outfit she was going to wear in the first place. Feminine yet strong. Original, yet not too funky. The sling, however, nearly ruined the look. Gillian rummaged through a few hat boxes of accessories and came up with a long white scarf scattered with tiny red dots. Using her teeth and her good arm, she managed to tie it. She slipped it over her shoulder then ducked her head to get it around her neck.

"Better," Gillian said to her reflection in the mirror. She was making some minor adjustments to the scarf when out on the street a horn honked. She ran to the window and looked out. An enormous old hulk of a car, the color of lemons, waited at the curb. Gillian smiled. Yes, Philo Hernshaw would own such a car.

She ran down the stairs, went out the front door and got into her lawyer's car.

"You're so sweet to pick me up," she said. "It's such a nuisance not being able to drive."

"My pleasure, Miss Plane."

"Um—that's Caine, Mr. Hernshaw."

"What? Oh, no. I don't use a cane. Although I think they can sometimes add a touch of distinction to a gentleman."

"No, Mr. Hernshaw. My name is—"

There was the blare of a horn and the squeal of tires as Philo Hernshaw edged the car into traffic and Gillian decided it was best not to bother him while he was driving.

Philo Hernshaw was a sweet man, very courtly, with crisp white hair, a short little beak of a nose and pale blue eyes. He dressed impeccably in suits that could have come from the kind of vintage clothing shops Gillian loved to rummage in—though, in Philo Hernshaw's case, Gillian was fairly certain that the suits were strictly one-owner. In all the social graces, her lawyer was quite acceptable. But Gillian was a little dubious of his mental powers. Oh, he didn't seem senile—exactly. He was just a bit vague. Most of the time he had a secret little smile on his faded lips—like he was experiencing a pleasant memory—but every once in a while he'd sort of get this look on his face like he wasn't sure how he'd gotten where he was at that particular moment. Very unsettling.

There was another blare of car horns as Philo made a turn onto Ludington Avenue without using his blinker. His driving wasn't exactly instilling any more confidence. Unfortunately, he was the only lawyer within one hundred miles of Timber Bay willing to take her case. Gillian suspected his appointment book wasn't exactly jammed.

Tires squealed as Philo changed lanes and Gillian decided to spend the rest of the trip with her eyes closed. Luckily, the courthouse was only about a mile down Ludington Avenue—right across the street from the hospital Lukas had taken her to—and they managed to arrive alive and unscathed.

Ever the gentleman, Philo came around and opened the door for her, offered his arm, and escorted her up the long walk that led to the courthouse.

"Quite a day, isn't it, Miss Spain?"

Gillian opened her mouth to correct him, but decided to merely agree. "Yes, Mr. Hernshaw. It's a beautiful day."

The morning was sunny with a gentle breeze that stirred the gold-and-red leaves on the trees that dotted the grounds of the lovely little redbrick courthouse. The building was done in the federalist style, complete with an American flag flying from the top of its petite white rotunda.

It was all so bucolic. So undisturbed looking. Gillian felt a twinge in her belly that had nothing to do with those half-dozen sweet buns and everything to do with the fact that she was about to disturb this bucolic scene—big-time.

Philo held the door for her and she walked into the cool, dim marble foyer. There was a small group of people at the other end. Despite the fact that her eyes hadn't fully adjusted to the dimness, Gillian immediately recognized Lukas by height and breadth alone. He was grinning at a short middle-aged woman with a pretty face and neat dark hair who was reaching up and trying to push back those loose curls that fell over his forehead. His mother, no doubt. The man standing next to her, a graying, slightly shorter version of Lukas, had to be his father. Molly was there, too, smiling and teasing her brother about their mother's ministrations.

Gillian felt an unexpected pang of loneliness at the sight of McCoy's family gathered around him. They all looked so nice. They reminded her of her own family. Well, minus the four brothers she had and plus the sister she'd always wanted.

As they approached, something made Lukas look up and the smile on his face, the one that deepened his dimples enough for a girl to get lost in them, totally disappeared.

Gillian sighed. "You are now entering the no-smile zone," she said under her breath.

"Did you say something, Miss Flame?" Philo asked.

Gillian winced. She was about to go up against one of the town's favorite sons and she had a lawyer who couldn't even get her name straight. Despite the fact that

Gillian firmly believed she was right in what she was doing, she didn't feel real terrific about it at the moment.

Luckily, just as Gillian's heart was warming to the McCoys—just as she started to wonder if she should just call the whole thing off—she heard the muffled sound of fabric rending as the back seam on the fitted bodice of her dress gave. And that made her remember the sweet-bun sabotage. Which made her remember the ruined pants and the damaged boot and her sprained arm. So when Molly came forward and started to introduce her parents, Gillian held up her good arm and yelled, "Stop!"

"Stop?" Molly inquired with a puzzled frown on her face.

"Please—just don't come any closer. Every encounter I've had with a McCoy since I came back to town has turned out badly. So please—just stay right where you are until I'm safely inside the courtro—"

Gillian didn't get to finish. There was a commotion behind the courtroom doors and then they burst open and an elderly man in a black robe came running out.

"Bees!" he yelled.

"What?" squawked Gillian.

"Bees!" the court reporter, hot on the heels of the judge and gripping her little machine in her hands, yelled.

"Close the doors!" someone shouted, but it was too late. The foyer was already buzzing.

"Oh, my— I'm allergic," Philo said quite calmly just as a huge bumblebee landed on his nose. "Oh, my," he merely said again as he went cross-eyed looking at it. "I'm allergic, you know," he repeated politely.

The bee sat there quivering slightly as if it was trying to choose a pore to plunge its stinger into and Philo just stood there looking cross-eyed, so Gillian did the only thing she could think of. She swatted at the bee on Philo's nose.

As it turned out, swatted might have been too mild a

term because Philo went down like a felled tree with the squished remains of the bee hanging off of his nose.

Lukas rushed over and crouched next to Philo's inert form. "Did the bee get him?"

"I don't know! I'm not sure!" Gillian cried, feeling perfectly awful as she peered at her lawyer over McCoy's hulking shoulder.

Lukas shook him but Philo remained stubbornly inert.

"Do you think he's in shock from bee venom?" Lukas's mother asked.

"I think it's more likely the princess punched his lights out," Lukas answered. "But just in case, we better get him to the hospital."

"Somebody call 911!" Gillian shouted, but Lukas was already picking the lawyer up off the floor.

"The hospital is right across the street. I'll take him."

"I'll come along," Molly said.

Gillian stood there with her mouth hanging open as Lukas carried her lawyer out the door, cradling him in his arms like he was no more than a child.

"Swell," Gillian said. "There goes my lawyer and the defendant. Talk about odd couples."

"Doesn't matter," the judge said. "No courtroom, anyway. There was a whole damn nest of bees under the bench."

Gillian panicked. The hearing couldn't be postponed! Because if it was, it would mean that she was going to fail in business once again.

She grabbed ahold of the judge's robe. "But Judge, you don't understand! We have to have this hearing today! I could lose my business if we don't."

The judge sized her up, his lined face scrunching and his eyes squinting. "You prepared to act as your own lawyer?"

"Lukas is acting as his own lawyer," Mr. McCoy said. Mrs. McCoy nodded in agreement.

Gillian, who'd gotten hooked on the courtroom show that gave her the idea to sue McCoy in the first place, figured if Lukas McCoy could be his own lawyer, so could she. "Yes!" she answered, bobbing her head up and down enthusiastically.

"Then find me a courtroom, girlie, and we're in business."

Gillian was ecstatic and didn't wonder until much later at the wisdom of wanting to go before a judge who called her *girlie.*

She was pacing, trying to come up with an idea for an alternative courtroom when the doors to the main entrance burst open and a group of women came bustling in, each of them carrying a weird-looking plant in their hands.

"We were over in the church basement, Judge," a pleasant-looking middle-aged woman said, "for our weekly quilting club, when we heard you had an insect problem."

"Bees, Kate," the judge said. "Damn courtroom hasn't been used in so long that a bunch of 'em built a nest right up there under the bench."

"Oh, dear. I don't know if my carnivores like bees. But I haven't had a chance to feed them yet today so I know they're hungry."

"Feed them?" Gillian asked.

"Dead flies, dear," Kate said sweetly. "My babies love them."

Gillian didn't quite know what to say to the woman with the chomping plant. Luckily Lukas came back and she went rushing up to him for a report on Philo.

"Is he all right?"

"Yup. Molly is staying with him until they finish in the emergency room. You knocked him out cold. His nose is turning purple already. I guess I should be glad you're taking me to court and not beating the hell out of me, huh, princess?"

Gillian's mouth dropped open. "You know it was an accident, McCoy. Besides, I might have saved his life. For all you know that bee was getting ready to plunge his stinger into poor addled Mr. Hernshaw."

"Next time, princess, try just swatting it away."

There was a twinkle in his eye and for a moment Gillian thought he was going to smile at her. She found herself waiting for it, hoping for it, like she'd waited as a kid to see what a neighbor was going to drop into her sack on Halloween.

Apparently, she was still in the no-smile zone because it didn't come. Instead he turned to the quilting ladies. "You ladies aren't going in there with all those bees loose. If anyone is taking those things into that courtroom, it's gonna be me."

Gillian glared at him. Whittler to the rescue, again—and making a good impression on the judge at the same time.

Gillian stepped in front of Lukas and stopped him with the flat of her hand on his chest. Oh, my. And a very hard chest it was, too. She pulled her hand off of it before she forgot what she was going to say.

"You're not going in there, either, McCoy. You're not disappearing on any more rescue missions until I get my day in court."

"You're forgetting, princess, we don't have a courtroom unless we get rid of the bees."

"Or find a temporary substitute," the judge added.

"What about the church basement?" Kate Walker suggested.

LUKAS SAT on a little chair meant for a Sunday-school student in the basement of the Church of the Holy Flock and wondered whose side Kate Walker was on. She was the mother of his best friend and partner. Why was she so all-fired eager to get him sued? Lukas wouldn't have minded putting the whole thing off for another month when the judge came around again. And he sure as heck would not have minded having a full-size chair to sit on. But with the Church of the Holy Flock quilting club running overtime due to their thwarted *carnivores to the rescue* attempt and the choir refusing to postpone their practice and the Christmas bazaar committee meeting also taking place, there was a shortage of chairs. The judge got the last full-size folding chair in the place. Lukas's lucky father got to lean on the wall and his mother had joined the rest of the quilters at the back of the room—no doubt tickled that she didn't have to miss a club meeting, after all, just because her son was being sued.

Lukas shifted slightly in his seat, trying to keep his butt from going to sleep, and hoped to heck the dinky wooden chair didn't break beneath him. All he needed was to appear the fool again in front of the big-city princess who, at that very moment, was standing there in that pretty red dress with her arm in a sling and a wounded look in those big eyes, telling her story to the judge. Lukas figured it was a shoo-in that he was gonna lose this case.

Maybe his mom had been right when she'd scolded him about the accident. Even though he was paying Gillian's doctor bills, his mom thought that he should have gone over to the dress shop and offered his services until her arm healed. He hadn't wanted to point out that he didn't do so well around Gillian, so he'd just scoffed at the idea.

"Your turn, McCoy," the judge said.

"Huh?" Lukas asked.

"Let's hear your side, boy."

"Oh."

Lukas tried to rise from the desk without much luck. He decided the best thing to do was to slide to the floor and stand up from there. When he did, the quilters erupted into giggles. He flashed a look at them in time to see his ma try to wipe the smile off her face. Swell. He expected to be laughed at by the likes of Ina Belway, who ran Belway's Burgers and Brews, or Clara, who ran the lunch counter down at Ludington Drugs. But his mom?

"The court is waiting," the judge said.

Yeah, he felt like saying, and so is the quilting club.

"What she says is true, Judge. I did come up out of that manhole without any warning, but it's not real bright to stand on one in the first place, is it?"

"Point taken. So you think it's all the plaintiff's fault?"

"Well, no. Not exactly."

"Then how much would you say is your fault?"

"Well, I'd be willing to take fifty percent of the blame, Judge. I'm already paying her doctor bills."

"That point also taken, McCoy. Nevertheless, taking into consideration the income Miss Caine stands to lose if her store isn't ready to open in time, I'd say doctor bills aren't going to cover it."

Lukas's heart sank beneath visions of selling his truck, selling his house, selling his—

"But," the judge went on, "I sure don't want to see you go broke. So here's what I'm going to do." He turned to Gillian. "It seems to me that what you need, girlie, is what women have always needed. A man. So that's what I'm giving you."

The quilters gasped and Gillian said, "Excuse me?"

"No point in awarding money damages when I know that Lukas here doesn't have much. But what he does have is a strong back and two arms that work. So I'm awarding you Lukas McCoy, girlie."

Gillian jumped to her feet. "But Your Honor, I don't want him."

The quilting club laughed outright at that and the choir, practicing in the room above them, could be heard to sing out, "Hallelujah!"

"Well, you're getting him anyway, girlie. Blame is split

even, far as I'm concerned. Therefore, taking into consideration that a usual day's work is eight hours, I'm sentencing Lukas McCoy to work for four hours a day helping you get that store of yours ready to open."

"But Your Honor! I never want to go near a McCoy again. So far they've ruined an expensive pair of boots and an original pair of—"

"You planning on seeking damages for those things, too?" the judge asked.

"Well, no, it's just that—"

"Then you've got Lukas McCoy for four hours a day until the doc says the sling can come off. Since this is Friday, he can start serving his sentence on Monday. Case closed."

Gillian gasped and looked at Lukas with horror in her big gray eyes.

And above them the choir repeated, "Halleeeeluuuujaaaah!"

JUST BEFORE SIX on Monday evening, Lukas came out the front door of the Sheridan Hotel, a toolbox tucked under one arm, and looked around to see if anyone was watching before he crossed the street to the dress shop. He decided to go around back rather than stand at the front door to the shop, waiting to be let in. Just because the whole town knew he was going to be paying his debt to society by working in a dress shop didn't mean he wanted any witnesses to the event.

He had to knock a couple of times before Gillian opened the door. When she did, he got a surprise. The big-city princess was wearing faded jeans and a big flannel shirt, tied at the waist. She seemed even shorter than he remembered. He looked down at her feet. Barefoot. That was why.

"The prisoner has arrived," she said. "Come on in."

Prisoner? Lukas was all for being humble but he wasn't

going to stoop to being Gillian Caine's prisoner—or anyone else's for that matter. "I think the word the judge used was *award*," Lukas told her. "You're looking at your winnings, princess."

"An award is something that gets put on a shelf, McCoy. I prefer the term slave. Now let's get to work."

She led him through the workroom—a clutter of sewing machines, fabric, and colorful things on hangers—and into the shop itself.

"The first thing I want you to do is to hang these mirrors on the wall behind the sales counter. And then—"

Lukas was barely listening. "What in the heck happened to the woodwork in this place?"

"I stained it pink." She had a proud little grin on her face. "Very effective, don't you think?"

"But the wood and crown moldings are solid oak!" he protested.

Gillian shrugged. "They were too dark. I'm going for more of a French look so I—"

"And what did you do to the front door?" Lukas felt sick at heart as he looked at the old door with its deeply carved garlands of flowers.

"I whitewashed it."

"Too dark, I suppose?"

She cocked her head and studied him for a moment with her big eyes. "Oh, I get it," she said. "You're one of those people that think bare wood is sacred."

"I just don't see the point in covering up beauty—"

"Enhancing it. I'm enhancing the beauty of the wood. That's why I stained and whitewashed instead of painted. You can see the wood grain through it." She ran her hand over the door and he was surprised that her nails were bare and ragged. Like the hands of a working woman. "And now the worn and damaged parts look more interesting."

"You did all this work yourself?"

She nodded and he could see the pride and happiness in her eyes. They were shining as bright as her fall of ash-colored hair.

But Lukas still didn't like people covering up wood. "Show me where you want the mirrors," he said gruffly, heaving his toolbox up onto the sales counter.

When he finished with the mirrors, she had a sign she wanted hung on the dressing-room door. It was all fancy with flowers and stuff painted on it and some sort of foreign language scrawled on it in ornate letters.

"What's it say?" Lukas asked.

"It says *Dressing Room* in French."

"I hate to break it to you, princess, but not many people in Timber Bay know French."

She flapped a hand. "Oh—that doesn't matter."

"Heck, of course it matters. How do you expect people to be able to read it?"

She looked exasperated. "Well, it's *obvious* that that," she said, gesturing at the swinging, louvered doors, "is a dressing room. I mean, what else would it be?"

"Then why have a sign at all?"

Gillian gave an exaggerated sigh and rolled her eyes. "Just hang it, okay? And then I've got some furniture upstairs you can bring down for me."

She headed for the back room again. Lukas watched her walk away. The rear of her jeans was worn nearly clear through. They weren't too tight, but they fit her round bottom nicely and he liked the way the tied shirt showed off her hips. She was more curvy than he'd thought. He liked that in a woman. He started to smile, but she looked over her shoulder. Quickly he dipped his head and lost the smile while pretending to look for something in his toolbox.

When Lukas had hung the sign, Gillian took him upstairs, showed him the two chairs in the living room that she wanted moved downstairs, then left him to it. Once he'd carried the chairs downstairs, she had trouble deciding where to put them so he ended up moving them, here, there and everywhere. Twice.

When she asked him to lug them back over near the dressing room for the third time, he said, "Heck, what do you need these for, anyway? It's a dress shop. People come. They look. They buy or they don't. What do they need to sit down for?"

"All the boutiques in New York offer places to sit," she said while she squatted to fuss with the ruffled skirt on one of the chairs. "Some even offer light refreshments. Like tea. I'm thinking of offering tea."

"This isn't New York City. The women around here shop and go home. They don't sit around drinking tea in stores."

Satisfied with the ruffle, she stood up. "Exactly the point, McCoy. I intend to give the women of Timber Bay the kind of shopping experience they've never had before. They deserve an alternative to Whittaker's Department Store, the dime store and the discount store out on the highway. And I'm going to give it to them. Now let's try the chairs over by the dressing room again, please."

He lugged them over. They were little things—padded and covered with flowered shiny stuff, the kind of chair he'd seen in ladies' bedrooms in old movies—but they weighed half a ton. Must have frames of solid wood. He stood back while Gillian angled them this way and that until she was satisfied.

"Perfect," she said as she stood back to look at them. "This way, if a woman comes in with her husband or boyfriend, he can sit and wait for her to come out of the dressing room and show him what she's trying on."

Oh, yeah. Lukas could just see his dad sitting around waiting for his mom to try on clothes. Heck, Danny was nuts about Hannah, but even Danny would never hang around in a place like this waiting for her to decide what to buy. He shook his head. "Timber Bay doesn't grow those kind of sissy men, princess."

"Sissy, huh?" She looked at him like she was trying to figure out what made him tick. "So you wouldn't be interested in anything your girlfriend buys to put on her body?"

It had been a while since Lukas had had a girlfriend. The women he fell for tend to leave Timber Bay as soon as they had saved enough money to go. Lukas had never cared enough about any of them to give up his hometown, his family or his best friend.

Not see little Chloe grow up? Not be here to shovel his parents' walk when they got too fragile to do it? Not be around to play big brother to Molly? Not plan and dream and scheme with Danny? He saw all these people every day of his life. And that's the way he intended to keep it. So no, he wouldn't leave Timber Bay for a woman.

And he wouldn't sit around on some flowered chair and wait for her to try on dresses, either.

"Men don't shop with women," he said. "At least I don't. Seems to me you could put the space to better use than cluttering it up with a couple chairs nobody is going to use anyway."

She put her hands on her hips and looked up at him, her gray eyes flashing a shade darker. "Look, McCoy, you're supposed to work off your sentence, not critique everything I'm doing."

"Well, maybe if you were doing anything right I wouldn't have to critique it."

She set her jaw and poked him in the chest with her finger. "Just keep it up, McCoy, and I'll get the judge to impose a gag order."

"Gag is exactly what the quilting club is going to do when they get a load of this," Lukas said as he grabbed something orange with huge ruffles from a hook near the dressing room and held it up. He wasn't at all sure what it was supposed to be. "I can see why you're calling the place Glad Rags."

Gillian snatched it out of his hands. "Like you know anything about fashion."

"I know what looks good on a woman," he retorted. And right now he couldn't help but notice, despite their arguing, that the flannel shirt Gillian was wearing looked damn good on her. It was worn and soft and it slid gently over the swell of her breasts as she moved. The heat of anger on her cheeks and the flash of it in her gray eyes looked pretty good on her, too.

"You probably prefer your women covered in sawdust and wood chips," she retorted with a toss of her head.

"Well, that would look a damn sight better than that silver spacesuit you were wearing the other day."

She gasped and a brief wave of hurt washed over her eyes. "I designed that ensemble myself," she said, then turned around and stormed on back to the workroom and, for the first time that night, slammed the door shut behind her.

Lukas threw the hammer down onto the floor. What in the heck was the matter with him? He wasn't the kind of guy who generally found fault. He didn't pick things apart much. But the princess seemed to have some weird sort of effect on him. It made him jumpy. And the jumpiness only made him act worse. Good thing Gillian Caine wasn't likely to remain in Timber Bay for long. If the spacesuit and the orange ruffles were examples of what she was going to be selling, nobody was going to be buying. He predicted that she'd be taking her rags back to New York City before the first snowfall.

But in the meanwhile, it wouldn't kill him to try to be civil.

He dug a bag out of his toolbox, headed for the back of the shop, and knocked on the door to the workroom. "Gillian?"

She pulled the door open with such force that it bounced off the wall with a bang. "I don't think the judge said anything about us having to actually speak to each other," she shot at him, tossing her head. "So I'd appreciate it if you wouldn't. Speak to me, that is."

She was looking so much like that snotty little girl who used to visit her aunt that it almost made him want to smile but he chomped it down and decided to go formal.

"Can I speak to you long enough to apologize and offer you one of Molly's cinnamon buns?" he asked, holding up the bag.

Gillian looked at the bag and felt like swooning. She hadn't worked up the nerve to go back into Sweet Buns, but she'd been craving a cinnamon bun. Absolutely craving one.

"You want one?" Lukas asked.

Gillian hesitated. She should just tell him to shove his buns and slam the door in his face. But it was no use, she was in the throes of gourmand lust. "Well—only if you think you can spare one," she answered as nonchalantly as possible, all the while hoping the frosting hadn't stuck to the bag.

"I think I can spare one," he said.

She stood back and let him into the workroom.

They perched on stools at the long worktable that took up one whole wall. Lukas opened the bag and held it out to her.

"Help yourself," he said.

"Thanks." She took a bun and bit into it. Heaven. Practically day-old and yet it was still a celestial experience. She devoured the whole thing in three bites.

"Wow. I didn't know fashion types from New York City ate like that."

She grimaced. "They don't. And I usually try not to. But for some reason your sister's cinnamon buns are irresistible."

"I get that way about them, too," he said. "You know how they're really good?"

"How?"

"Warmed in the microwave. Did Aunt Clemintine have one?"

"Are you kidding? Her television is black-and-white. But we're in luck anyway, because I brought a microwave with me. Let's go."

She forgot to be nervous or uptight about his disapproval as they ran up the stairs and stuck the buns in the microwave.

They came out gooey and soft and filled the kitchen with a yeasty, fresh-baked aroma. Gillian pulled off a hunk of bun and popped it into her mouth.

"Hmm."

"Told ya," he said. And then he smiled at her. A full, two-dimpled grin that lit up his face like a kid who'd just scored a touchdown.

"You smiled," she said, totally bemused at the sight. "You smile at everyone else all the time, but this is the first time you've ever smiled at me."

Lukas shook his head and laughed. "No, that can't be true. I'm a smiley kind of guy."

"Yeah, I know. For the rest of the world. But around me you were always so solemn. So disapproving."

He ducked his head down and chewed for a while and she thought maybe she shouldn't have said anything about his smile because now it was gone. But then he looked at her again and grinned. "I approved of that white dress you were wearing the other night," he said.

"You did?"

He nodded. "You looked like a heap of stardust fallen from the sky."

It was several heartbeats before Gillian could answer. "That's a sweet thing to say," she said. "Really sweet."

"Is the dress all right? Was it damaged?"

"No, it's not damaged. In fact, it's going into the display window for the opening."

"I'm glad."

They sat there with melted frosting on their fingers, gazing into each other's eyes, while Aunt Clemintine's old kitchen clock ticked and the ancient refrigerator's motor kicked in. Gillian had an urge to reach out and smooth the hair off his brow like she'd seen his mother do at the courthouse. What sort of magic was this? Only a short time ago they'd been sparring like a couple of little kids. And now he was smiling at her and she was getting as gooey and warm inside as the frosting on a sweet bun.

"Gillian?" he said.

"Yes?"

"I really am sorry about what happened to your arm."

"Oh."

Wasn't McCoy supposed to be the laconic one? But here she was, reduced to single syllables. It was the dimples. She was getting lost in them. And the mouth. Yeah, she'd like to get lost in that. And his eyes. Warm and brown and soft. She reached up and smoothed the hair off his brow—but she didn't feel in the least like his mother.

When her fingertips grazed his forehead she heard him take in a breath. And then he was leaning closer. And then she was standing up. And he was sliding off the stool and reaching for her at the same time. And then—

"Aeiiiii!" Gillian screamed as Lukas's foot came down on hers.

"Oh, man, I did it again!" Lukas said in a voice that she could only describe as anguish laced with self-loathing. Something fluttered in her chest and she rushed to reassure him.

"It's not your fault—really—I shouldn't walk around barefoot."

"It's me—I've got that bull in the drugstore thing," he said as he dropped to his knees and gently lifted her foot.

His hands were warm and his touch was gentle.

"Can you wiggle your toes?" he asked.

She wiggled.

"Can you stand on it?"

"Um—you'll have to let go of it before I can find out."

"Oh—right." Gently, he lowered her foot back to the floor. Gingerly, Gillian put weight on it.

"It's okay," she said, letting out a swoosh of breath in relief.

"You're sure?"

Gillian was tempted to lie just to keep him kneeling at her feet like that. Such a sight. A big man brought to his knees. Of course, she'd had to risk another limb to get him there.

Wait a minute. Did she want him there?

And more importantly. Did he want to be there? Because the way he was looking up at her made her think that maybe he—

He cleared his throat and stood up. "I guess you were right. McCoys are dangerous to you."

Gillian felt a whole new kind of danger humming through her body and it had nothing at all to do with damaged limbs.

"I still have an hour of today's sentence to go," he said. "I better get back to work."

She felt a little sad when he left the kitchen and went back downstairs. It didn't help that he took the rest of the sweet buns with him.

4

GILLIAN STOOD on the sidewalk in front of Glad Rags and took in a big gulp of fresh air. The day was golden—and so was her mood. She hadn't even weighed herself that morning, despite the impromptu cinnamon bun pig-out session with Lukas the night before. If she'd gained a pound or two, it was worth it.

Because Lukas McCoy had smiled at her.

Finally.

She looked across the street at Sweet Buns. If Lukas had smiled at her, did that mean that she no longer had to worry whether Molly would welcome her as a customer or not? Her taste buds had done plenty of reminiscing about that chicken salad sandwich with apricot chutney she'd eaten there in her pretrial days. It was doubtful, though, that Lukas would have rushed to a phone as soon as he left last night to tell his sister that Gillian was no longer the enemy. With one last, longing look at Sweet Buns, she turned and headed for Ludington Drugs.

Despite the fact that apricot chutney wasn't at the end of her journey, Gillian enjoyed the walk. Autumn was supposed to be an ending—a last gasp before the death of winter. But Gillian had never seen it that way. To her it seemed hopeful, a promise that, although things were constantly changing, every season had its own gift to give. That was exactly how she was feeling about her life today. Everything seemed possible once again. The shop was shaping up. It looked like she'd be ready to open for the Harvest Festival. True, Glad Rags wasn't the boutique she'd always hoped to have in Manhattan, but it was hers and she was still designing, still working at what she loved to do.

And Lukas McCoy had smiled at her last night.

And almost kissed her. Yes, she decided as she walked past Cook's Furniture Store. Lukas had definitely been about to kiss her when he trod on her foot. Absolutely. Gillian could always tell when a man was about to kiss her—she felt it in her body. And last night, her body had definitely felt it—had been maneuvering in place for it, in fact. Unfortunately, her foot got in the way. And then afterwards, Lukas had gone back to work, all shy once again. She hadn't been able to coax more conversation out of him for the rest of the night, but at quitting time he'd given her a good-night and a sweet grin that followed her all the way up into bed and into her dreams.

At the corner, she waited for the light to change then crossed Ludington Avenue and went into the drugstore.

Scents clashed and blended. Perfume and the unmistakable smell of old-fashioned face powder from the cosmetic counter. Cough drops and that weird aroma that always came along with vitamins, or anything else in capsules, from the pharmacy. Bacon, hamburgers and coffee from the lunch counter. The sounds were just as varied and chaotic. All together, it was a very stimulating blend and it sent Gillian's appetite soaring.

She took a seat at the counter and a woman in an adorable pink-and-white uniform with the name Clara embroidered on the breast pocket slapped a one-page menu down in front of her.

"Special today is tuna on toast," she said. "You want coffee?" Gillian nodded and the waitress filled a cup and slid it in front of her before she went to take another order three stools down.

Tuna on toast couldn't quite compete with the chicken salad sandwich from Sweet Buns. Neither could the coffee, Gillian decided when she'd taken a sip. Not awful, but certainly not good, she thought as she reached for the cream—generally a diet no-no but in this case it was ulcer prevention, pure and simple.

If she didn't savor the coffee, she savored the buzz all around her as she sipped. The clink of glass and silverware, the buzz of conversation between the customers, the cook and waitress yelling back and forth.

"Special with a side of fries," the cook yelled.

"That was a side of slaw," Clara yelled back.

"Hell if it was…."

The argument joined the cacophony of sounds and Gillian sighed happily. If she closed her eyes, she could almost be back in New York in her favorite diner. She was floating pleasantly on nostalgia when the person who'd just sat down next to her said, "Aren't you the girl who sued Lukas McCoy?"

The cacophony of noise stopped with mortifying abruptness.

"You might not remember me," the woman went on like she hadn't noticed that all heads had turned their way. "I'm Kate Walker," she said pleasantly. "I'm the one who suggested the church basement for the trial."

The woman had such a sweet, open manner that it was hard to be annoyed at the unfortunate moniker she'd bestowed on Gillian. "Yes—yes, of course I remember you," Gillian said pleasantly. "You have the—um—meat-eating plants."

Kate smiled sweetly. "How nice. You do remember. This is my daughter-in-law, Hannah. Hannah, this is the girl who sued Lukas."

Gillian winced. Was that how she was going to be known from now on? The girl who sued Lukas McCoy?

As a testimonial, it stunk. *Where did you get that dress, Martha? At that little shop on Sheridan Road—the one owned by the girl who sued Lukas McCoy.* Her entrepreneurial heart shuddered at the thought.

"How is your arm?" Hannah asked. "Is it still painful?"

Gillian pulled her attention away from the awful scenario in her head and leaned forward so she could see the young woman on the other side of Kate Walker. "It still hurts but not nearly as bad as at first." She extended her good arm and offered her hand. "I'm Gillian," she said loud enough for the entire lunch counter to hear. She followed it with a pointed but mild gaze down the line of diners until someone coughed and the clanging of silverware and chattering of voices rose up again to cover the sound of whatever was sizzling in the little kitchen behind the counter.

"Small towns," Hannah whispered with a smile. "You get used to it."

"Promise?" Gillian asked.

Hannah laughed lightly. "Absolutely. I've only been here since June and I'm completely used to it already."

"Hannah is my son Danny's bride," Kate put in.

Hannah blushed like the newlywed she was and Gillian felt the slight sting of jealousy. Not long ago, she would have sworn that she and Ryan had an altar in their future. As it turned out, she hadn't even managed to hang on to him until the holiday sales. Which she'd had some spectacular ideas for. Well, never mind, she told herself. Timber Bay was going to benefit from her brilliant mind.

She dragged her focus back to Danny Walker's wife. "You're blushing," she teased. "You must be crazy about him."

"They're just made for each other," Kate Walker gushed while she patted Hannah's hand. And a more sincere gush Gillian had never seen. "We love having her in the family."

Hannah gave Kate a smile of genuine fondness and Gillian wondered what her story was. Danny Walker's bride was dressed in classic preppy fare—chinos, white shirt, good but subdued light wool blazer. She looked smart, both fashion-wise and brain-wise. Certainly not a woman you'd pick out at a party as having arrived on the arm of Danny Walker.

Clara came over and Gillian glanced quickly at the menu and ordered a BLT. Hannah ordered three cheeseburgers to go—and one tuna special on white bread, untoasted.

Clara chuckled and shook her head. "That Lukas," she said as she wrote down the order. "Most people get a side of fries or slaw. Lately he gets a tuna on white with every order."

Gillian felt a little jolt in her chest—and she didn't think it was because of the gastronomic faux pas of having tuna on white and a cheeseburger at the same meal.

"Gillian, get a hold of yourself," she murmured in disgust. "This isn't high school."

"Excuse me, dear? Did you say something?" Kate asked.

"Oh—um— I just said this place reminds me of a place I used to go to in high school."

Kate smiled sweetly. "That's nice, dear," she said, then went back to telling Clara that she just wanted coffee while she waited for a prescription. The pocket of solitude gave Gillian time enough to rethink the night before—and suddenly she was very glad that the kiss hadn't happened.

What a dope. Practically skipping down the street 'cause the big lug had smiled at her. Her heart doing somersaults at the mere mention of his name. Totally disgusting. Hadn't she learned anything from Ryan fever? Falling in love was losing control of your life. The last thing she needed was to fall in love again. Huh! They should call it *falling out of control* because that's exactly what happened.

She was glad that it looked like she and Lukas were going

to be able to work together without killing each other, but that was all. And if he thought that his sentence was coming with conjugal rights, well, he was going to be very—

"Hey, aren't you the girl who sued Lukas McCoy?"

Gillian winced before reluctantly swiveling around on her stool. The woman was middle-aged and lean, wearing a suit that looked like a wardrobe reject from a nineteen-forties B movie. She had a cigarette hanging out of the side of her mouth and lipstick on her front teeth.

"Gillian," Kate said sweetly, "this is Gertie Hartlet. She owns the real estate agency in town. Gertie, this is Gillian Caine—you know, Clemintine's niece."

"The girl who sued Lukas McCoy," Gertie repeated.

"Well, yes—but only because—" Gillian began.

Gertie didn't seem to be paying attention as she ran her hand over the arm of the coatdress Gillian was wearing. "What's this made out of?" she asked around her cigarette.

Gillian fanned the smoke away and answered, "It's one of the new microfibers."

"This feels like my granny's flannel nightgown to me," Gertie said as she fingered the lapel.

"That's because I've lined the microfiber with good old-fashioned flannel—both for warmth and for fun and nostalgia. It's from my upcoming Urban Flannel Collection for winter," Gillian said brightly. As long as she had an audience, she might as well plug her line.

Gertie laughed, spewing a fresh cloud of smoke into Gillian's face. Gillian coughed and fanned but Gertie seemed oblivious. "You want fun, you're going to have to throw in a martini with every purchase. What's this thing gonna set a person back?"

Gillian stared in fascination as the glowing tip of the cigarette bobbed with every word Gertie uttered. "Um—excuse me?"

"What's it cost?"

"Oh—it's just under three hundred dollars."

Gertie gave a bark of laughter and Gillian inhaled enough smoke to blacken a lung. "Call me when you have your going-out-of-business sale, honey," Gertie said.

"Why, Gertie," Kate exclaimed. "That's just plain mean."

"I call it honest, Kate," Gertie rasped.

"Gertie, for heaven's sake, put out that cigarette before you kill us all," Clara snapped as she put Gillian's sandwich down in front of her. Gillian looked down at it and found that her appetite had dwindled along with all those possibilities she'd been feeling just minutes ago. "Would you mind wrapping this to go, Clara?" she asked. "I need to get back to work."

"Hey, Gertie, if you want that dress, maybe you better buy it now," someone from the far end of the counter called out. "Word is the Sheridan kid is coming back from Chicago with a couple of women on his arm. Three hundred bucks would be nothing to them."

"I'll take my chances," Gertie said.

When Clara handed her a take-out bag, Gillian was tempted to sock Gertie Hartlet in the head with it. Instead, she put some bills on the counter, slid off the stool, and wove her way through the aisles of dusting powder, vaporizers and greeting cards and out the front door. She crossed Ludington Avenue, then paused in the window of Cook's Furniture Store—not so much to admire the display of TV trays on sale, as to check out her reflection. She'd already rethought all her prices with the Midwesterner in mind. Was three hundred dollars still too much for the coatdress she was wearing?

She struck a pose and studied her reflection with a critical eye. The dress was impeccably tailored in the shoulders and chest, like fine men's wear, but there the similarity ended. The silhouette narrowed at the midriff to nip in at the waist and fit closely to the hips, then the fabric swirled out slightly down almost to the ankles, where it was finished off with a deep ruffle of red and black plaid flannel. The lapels and the French cuffs were cut from the same plaid flannel. She'd had enough flannel left over to fashion a sling. The effect, she thought, was rather jaunty.

No, she wasn't wrong about the dress. "Smashing," she murmured to her reflection. "The dress is smashing."

"Yes, it is."

Gillian whirled to find Hannah Walker watching her. She held up the take-out bags in her hands. "I'm walking down to the hotel to have lunch with Danny. If you're heading back to the dress shop, we can walk together."

Gillian shrugged. "Sure, why not." Might as well get it over with, she thought as she fell into step beside Danny Walker's wife. She fully expected Hannah to start berating her for suing Danny's partner, but what she said was, "It really is a spectacular dress. It's just that—"

"Price too steep?" Gillian asked, peering at Hannah sideways.

"I'm afraid it might be. On average, the women of Timber Bay don't spend more than one hundred dollars on a dress—and then only for something like a wedding or a funeral."

"A hundred dollars? But in Manhattan, I could get three times what I'm asking for it."

"Well," Hannah said reasonably, "in Manhattan, the median income is—"

Gillian held up her hand. "Please—I don't want to know what the difference is in median incomes. Don't dash all my dreams on our first walk together."

Hannah laughed. "Sorry. I used to be a research sociologist. My head is full of statistics, I'm afraid."

"What do you do now?" Gillian asked.

"Coming to Timber Bay sort of put me in touch with the left side of my brain. So I'm writing a novel. I also work part-time at the newspaper, writing obituaries and community news."

"Wow—you're not afraid of change. You must love Danny very much."

"Oddly enough, I do."

Gillian laughed. "You are sort of an odd couple."

"I'm well aware, believe me. And Timber Bay is just as different from the world of academia where I grew up as Danny and I are from each other."

"How on earth did you end up here?"

Hannah told Gillian about the contest she'd been running to find The Great American Family for Granny's Grains cereal *Bringing America Back to the Breakfast Table* campaign.

"And you found them in Timber Bay?" Gillian asked incredulously.

Hannah laughed. "The cereal company had exactly the same reaction to the Walker family."

"The Walkers? You're kidding, right? The woman with the flesh-eating plants is supposed to be a role model?"

"Kate is the most wonderful woman I ever met—but she steals dead flies from the neighbor's yard to feed to her babies, as she calls them, she hosts a weekly secret poker game for some of the ladies from The Church of the Holy Flock, and she lies about how much bourbon she puts in her mincemeat for pies. And the rest of the family is just as—well—as unique."

"Good word," Gillian said. "Very diplomatic."

"Thank you. After a few days with the Walkers, I started to lose faith in studies and statistics. They were nothing like they were supposed to be. But in the end, it didn't matter, because I decided that they were perfect just the way they were. Unfortunately, the CEO of Granny's Grains didn't see it that way. I lost the job—"

"But gained a husband," Gillian finished for her.

Hannah grinned. "Yeah, and a family and a hometown."

Gillian looked into Hannah's content face and wondered what it would be like to feel so accepted someplace. In suing Lukas, had she ruined her chance to have what Hannah had found?

Hell, the town hadn't been that fond of her before she'd taken Lukas to court. And now she was learning that despite the fact that she'd cut her prices, they were still too high for the style-challenged of Timber Bay. But hadn't someone at the lunch counter mentioned customers from Chicago?

"Hannah, someone at the drugstore mentioned some women coming here from Chicago. Do you get many tourists from Chicago?"

Hannah shook her head. "Not usually. Although we do attract a few tourists from across the bay in Door County. In the summer, they sail over for the day. Danny hopes that once the hotel is open, Timber Bay will see more. But the people they were talking about at the drugstore aren't tourists. Agnes Sheridan's grandson is coming back from Chicago and rumor has it that he's not coming alone."

"Coming back to stay, you mean? That's hard to believe."

"I know. Gavin Sheridan is head of the Sheridan Hotel chain, based in Chicago. I can't imagine him giving all that up. But Danny says that Mrs. Sheridan has been hoping that her grandson would come back if she restored the hotel."

"I take it that Danny wouldn't exactly be thrilled about that."

"Frankly, no. He wouldn't. Neither of them has apparently gotten over a boyhood rivalry. Which is somewhat silly but not all that uncommon. Statistics show—"

Gillian laughed. "Please. No statistics unless they're going to show me that Gavin Sheridan and his female companions will be in town at least long enough for them to do a little shopping." They'd reached Glad Rags. "Well, here we are. Guess I'll take my sandwich upstairs and—"

"Why don't you come over to the hotel with me?" Hannah asked. "Have you ever been inside?"

"No—no, I haven't."

"Then come and see it. You can eat with us."

"Us?"

"Danny and Lukas and me."

Gillian waited. No jolt. What a relief! "I'd love to see the hotel," she said, and realized that she meant it. Besides, it'd be good for business to cultivate a friendship with the wife of the partner of the man she sued.

Minutes later, Gillian was running her fingers along the vines carved on the front desk in the lobby of the Sheridan Hotel.

"Lukas did this?" she asked.

"That, plus the refurbishing of the banister," Danny said, nodding toward the staircase.

The staircase had a gorgeous sweep with the same pattern of vines festooning the banister that graced the front desk. She examined it again, running her fingers over the delicate vein of a leaf. "You can't even see where the original work ends and Lukas's begins."

Danny beamed. "Lukas is an artist."

"Is Lukas still working in the lounge?" Hannah asked.

"Yeah," Danny answered. "He's installing the new moldings he carved for the bar."

"Gillian, why don't you go find him and tell him his sandwiches are here," Hannah suggested. "It'll give you a chance to see him work."

"Hey—good idea," Danny said. "Lounge is just on the other side of the ballroom—through those French doors over there."

"Okay," Gillian said. "Be right back."

She went through the glass-paned doors and stopped short. "Wow," she gasped.

Light poured in through another set of French doors that stood open on the far side of the room and spilled across the white marble floor. The sky-blue paint on the high Spanish plaster walls was peeling and the crown moldings that outlined the domed ceiling were crumbling, but what a place it would be after dark, with candles lit in the sconces that rimmed the room and music from an unseen band playing. A waltz, she thought. She suddenly saw herself in the white dress—a heap of stardust, Lukas had called it—twirling about the floor, gazing up at her partner.

Who just happened to be Lukas in a tuxedo.

"Not good, Gillian," she murmured. For several reasons, including the fact that if a girl danced with Lukas McCoy she was sure to have a pair of crutches in her future.

She was still grinning at the thought when she pushed open the door to the lounge and found him kneeling before an ornate oak bar, caressing the carvings with his big hand. She stopped grinning and started breathing heavily instead.

He'd been on his knees before her last night, her injured foot in his hand. His touch had been sweet, but he hadn't caressed her foot with as much reverence as he touched the wood now. This time the jolt in her chest went right into her throat and curled into a lump.

Watching him work was like watching something intimate, private. But she couldn't stop. Until, from behind her, Danny said, "Oh, you found him."

Lukas started to grin as he looked up from the work he was doing on the antique bar. Then he saw Gillian and the grin froze midway.

He hadn't been able to stop thinking about her and now here she was, standing there looking like she just walked off the cover of one of those fashion magazines he'd seen down at the drugstore. The desert was in his mouth again and his tongue was not about to behave under those conditions. To avoid having to speak, he stood up and started to rummage in the toolbox on top of the bar.

Someone coughed and then Danny said, "Uh—lunchtime, pal."

When he kept rummaging, Hannah said, "I ran into Gillian at the drugstore and suggested she come back here and eat with us. Good idea, don't you think, *Lukas?*" she asked pointedly.

He couldn't exactly ignore Hannah—especially not when she was talking to him in that haughty voice that made her sound like she was a really strict grade schoolteacher—so Lukas looked up. But it wasn't Hannah he looked at.

The princess had red boots on today. The color of them matched the color on her mouth. To think he'd had the nerve to almost kiss that mouth last night. Because if he hadn't stepped on her foot, he thought with an inward wince, he would have had her in his arms—would have had his mouth on hers. Maybe it had been the flannel shirt or the bare feet that had made him for one second think she was the kind of girl that got kissed by a guy like him. Whatever it was, he figured stepping on her foot was less of a humiliation than how she would have reacted to him putting his rough hands on her like that. He wasn't going to be making that mistake today. In the bright sunshine, Lukas could see that she was far too glossy for a guy like him.

So he said, "I'm planning on working through lunch," and went back to banging around in his toolbox like he expected to find buried treasure.

"Obviously, Lukas doesn't think it's a good idea," Gillian said.

Lukas heard the click of her red boots walking away from him across the marble floor.

"Well, that was suave, pal," Danny said.

"Lukas, I've never seen you act that way before." Hannah stared at him with the kind of curiosity she'd give to a research subject. And why not? He'd just acted like a rat.

He slammed the lid of his toolbox. "How does she do that to me?"

"What? Turn you into a boorish jerk?" Danny asked.

"Damn!" Lukas raked his hand through his hair. "Looked just as bad as it felt, huh?"

"Yup. I won't lie to you. You weren't exactly charming."

"My damn tongue just turns stupid around her. It's not like me—you know that, Danny."

"True. I mean, you were never as smooth as I was, but you could hold your own with my cast-offs any day."

Hannah cleared her throat. "This is no time to crack jokes—and certainly no time to remind me how smooth you can be, Danny," she said in her schoolteacher voice. Then she turned to Lukas. "Have you ever considered, Lukas, that it might be the legend causing your problems around Gillian?"

Lukas frowned. "You mean the legend of the Tunnel of Love?"

"Exactly. Don't you remember, Danny? I resisted the obvious effects of the legend after the tunnel threw us together."

"Remember?" Danny laughed. "I've still got the scars, baby."

"Well, Lukas is doing the same thing."

"You're forgetting something, Hannah. The legend says that if the tunnel brings a man and a woman together, they are destined to fall in love for all time. But the tunnel didn't bring Gillian and Lukas together."

"But it did," Hannah insisted. "Lukas was coming out of the tunnel when he injured Gillian. The injury caused her to sue him. The judge sentenced Lukas to work for Gillian. Therefore—"

"I think she's got a point, Lukas," Danny interrupted. "In a roundabout way, the tunnel *has* brought you two together. And you sure as hell are resisting the effects."

"Aw," Lukas groaned, "that's the most ridiculous thing I've ever heard. And if I ever hear you repeat what you just said to another living person, I'm going to—"

"You're going to what, good buddy?"

Danny stood with his arm around Hannah. Both of them had grins on their faces. Lukas had never seen his partner look so happy. He'd never seen a woman look more in love. How was he supposed to stay mad at them for anything?

"Aw, never mind. Give me my tuna sandwich. Tiger is probably waiting for his lunch."

GILLIAN FED the last bit of bacon from her leftover sandwich to the battered old stray cat that had followed her home from the hotel that afternoon. He, at least, didn't seem to mind that she was the girl who sued Lukas McCoy.

At the moment Gillian was darn glad that she had taken the whittler to court. The nerve of the man, cutting her like that after he'd almost kissed her the night before! The fact that he'd done it in front of Danny and Hannah made her doubly mad. So now she was not only the girl who sued Lukas McCoy, she was the girl he ignored.

"Well, fine," she said to Pirate, the name she'd decided to call the stray because, with half his tail missing, he looked like he'd done his share of pillaging and looting. "It's just as well, really. The last thing I need is to have some kind of crush on a man right now. And that's all it would have been, you know—"

Pirate stopped licking a paw long enough to give her a veiled look of contempt.

"—well, it's true," she told the cat, making up her mind at that moment that it now belonged to her. "It was just a normal female reaction to an attractive man, that's all. But the last thing I need right now is to have a man in my life—as anything but a slave, that is. By the way," she said to Pirate as she got out some milk and a bowl, "remind me to tell you about Ryan some time."

She set the bowl down on the floor. Pirate regarded it under hooded lids.

"Yeah, I know," she grimaced, "it's skim. But it's all I've got."

Downstairs, someone pounded on the back door.

"The prisoner has arrived," Gillian said. Pirate looked bored with the idea so Gillian left him in the kitchen and ran down the steps to the workroom. She pasted a scowl on her face and threw open the back door. "You're late," she said, jerking her head toward the clock on the wall of the workroom. "Don't let it happen again or I'll have to report it."

Lukas scowled right back. "Two minutes," he said.

"Five," she retorted.

"So I'll stay five minutes later," he muttered. "What's the sentence for tonight, warden?"

She narrowed her eyes at him. So she'd gone from being a princess to being a warden. Okay, he wanted unpleasant, he was going to get unpleasant. Hmm, what would Lukas McCoy consider to be the worst job in the place? she wondered as she surveyed him. Aha, she thought almost immediately—the front window.

"Follow me, please."

Just as she thought, Lukas hated the idea of standing in the display window of the shop, hanging sheer pastel curtains. Gillian loved it when a couple of macho types walked by and hooted at him. He grumbled and muttered but, like a good boy, kept at the job she'd given him. But when she handed him a carton of lingerie and asked him to hang them on the huge branch she'd found in an alley and painted silver to resemble a futuristic tree, the whittler balked.

"You want me to what?" he asked, his boyish face screwed up in incredulity.

"I want you to decorate the tree with the lingerie in that carton."

He opened the carton and looked inside. "These are—um—" red color spread up his cheeks "—these are—uh—"

"Ladies' undies, McCoy."

"Look," he said, thrusting the carton at her, "when I signed up for this, nobody said I was gonna have to handle ladies'—uh—stuff."

"As I recall," she retorted, pushing the box back at him, "you didn't sign up. You were sentenced. Now get to work."

"Yes, warden," he grumbled, rummaging in the carton and coming out with a violet camisole. "You want *this* hanging from a branch in the window?"

"That's right, McCoy. Shake it out good first, though. You know, to sort of fluff up the fabric."

"Like this?" he asked, then caught sight of some people across the street. He hit the floor of the display window like he'd been shot.

Gillian bit her lip to keep from laughing. "McCoy, if you do that every time someone walks by, we'll never get any work done."

"That isn't just someone. That's Gavin Sheridan," Lukas said from his prone position.

"Really? He's back already?" Gillian leaned over Lukas's body to get a look. Oh, yes, the buzz at the lunch counter that afternoon had been right. The man standing in front of the Sheridan Hotel across the street looked as though he'd have no problem affording her prices. He was dark-haired and leanly elegant and that was definitely cashmere draping his shoulders. She couldn't really make out his features in the dim glow of an old-fashioned street lamp but he might as well have had a neon sign reading *class* hanging above him. Gillian tore her gaze off all that cashmere to check out the two women with him. Yes. Thin and rich. The neon above their heads blinked the words *potential customers.* "Hmm—at last," Gillian purred, "a sign of civilization."

"More like a sign of trouble," Lukas retorted.

"I thought Gavin Sheridan was *Danny's* enemy, not yours."

"I've never broken his nose but I wouldn't call myself a fan, either."

"Danny broke his nose?" Gillian grinned, not really sure why the thought satisfied her. It's not like she was on Lukas and Danny's team, for heaven's sake. She was still smiling when Gavin Sheridan turned and looked right at her. Even in this light, she could see that the broken nose hadn't ruined his looks. He nodded his head at her and saluted. She gave him a short, girly wave. No point in making an enemy. She didn't, after all, have to actually like her customers.

"What are you doing?" Lukas demanded from below.

"I'm waving at Gavin Sheridan," she said.

"Oh, swell. All I need is for him to take a stroll over here and see me lying on the floor, clutching women's underwear."

"Those are potential customers, McCoy. You're lucky I don't run out there and invite them in for a private showing."

"You do and I'll see to it that you never get another sweet bun as long as you live."

Loss of sweet buns—not something she took lightly. Luckily, it looked like it wasn't going to come to that. "Relax," she told Lukas, "they already went into the hotel."

"Come on, warden," he said, peering over the window ledge to make sure the coast was clear, "you must have something else for me to do."

"You mean something properly manly? Nope, sorry. This is what I need you to do tonight."

"Then at least close those practically useless curtains you made me hang."

"Oh—fine," Gillian grumbled as she swished the semi-sheer panels closed. "There. Now quit cowering on the floor like the macho police are after you and get back to work. If I want to start creating a buzz around town, this window has to start reflecting what Glad Rags is all about."

Lukas lumbered to his feet. "Huh—it's a cinch you don't have a clue what Timber Bay is all about," he muttered as he hung the camisole, then fished a gold lace demibra from the carton. "You can't just go hanging this kind of stuff in the window for everyone to see."

"You can see scantier stuff on the beach, McCoy."

"Not on any beach along Timber Bay, you can't," muttered Lukas.

She rolled her eyes. Like Timber Bay was any kind of arbiter of style. "The effect is going to be whimsical, not prurient. I'm going to have a fan hidden somewhere that will make the lingerie blow gently—and I'm going to have some tossed around at the foot of the tree, like leaves that have already fallen. And then, over there," she held out her arm toward the other side of the display area, "a mannequin will be wearing the white dress and a pink wool cape and a silver and pink witch hat—kind of saucily tilted over one eye. Hmm," Gillian mused, visualizing the vignette in her mind's eye, "maybe she should be holding a silver broomstick."

"This stuff isn't the right color if you're going for autumn leaves, princess."

Gillian sighed heavily. "Yes—and witch hats aren't pink, either, McCoy. It's called creative license."

He turned the scrap of lace over in his hand, examining

it with a puzzled frown on his face. It almost made Gillian want to laugh until she became fixated on his big hands and how gently they handled the wisp of gold. Something in the pit of her tummy knotted up. Gingerly, he hung the demibra from a branch, then plucked a silver and pink thong from the carton. The sight of the delicate scrap in his rough hands sent the knot in her tummy lower still. What would it be like to be touched through that cool, smooth silk with those rough, warm hands?

He smoothed his thumb over the delicately embroidered edging and Gillian started to ache.

This would never do.

"At this rate, we'll be here all night," she said—while her body screamed: *Like that would be a bad thing! Nope*, she told it. *Your life has been derailed by a man once. Never again.* In the interest of independence, Gillian made a grab for the thong. But the sling on her arm made her clumsy and she lost her balance and lunged toward Lukas, sending the carton of lingerie flying and the two of them tumbling. The brittle branches of the silver tree cracked like dry kindling on a bonfire, and bras and panties took flight like a colorful flock of frightened birds.

When the cracking and flying ended, Gillian found herself in a heap on the display window floor with Lukas lying on the bed of twigs that used to be her lingerie tree, half buried in a pile of silk and lace. Careful to protect her sprained arm, she struggled to her knees and crawled over to him.

"Lukas?" She tossed bras and panties aside until she found a nose sticking out of the leg of a French-cut lace panty. She picked it up and Lukas's brown eyes looked up at her.

"Are you all right?" she asked. His answer was muffled by a black lace thong that had inserted itself into his mouth like a gag. She plucked it off.

"Not exactly the way it's worn, McCoy," she said, grinning down at him.

"Maybe you'd like to demonstrate the right way to wear it, princess," he said, his mouth twisting like he was holding back a wicked grin.

"Like you're demonstrating how to wear that bustier, McCoy?" she asked, nodding at his head. "I'd say that noggin of yours is going to need at least a double D cup."

He burst out laughing. And wasn't it a wonderful laugh? Deep and rich and round. A man's laugh. She felt the heat and movement of it under her palm where it rested on his chest. He was wearing a bustier like a yarmulke and a bikini panty like an ear cuff, but he was all dimples and all man.

"And here I am on the ground again. I can't seem to stay upright when you're around, McCoy. You really are that bull in the drugstore."

He stopped laughing and shook his head. "Nope, princess. This one is all your fault."

"That's your story," she said as she reached out and pulled the bustier off his head, tossing it aside. Her fingers hovered and she knew what they wanted. So she reached out and smoothed the rumpled hair off his forehead.

Their gazes locked and Gillian started to get a strange, whirling sensation. Under her hand, she felt his heartbeat quicken.

Slowly, he started to rise up on one elbow.

Run, she told herself. Run like hell.

But when he threaded his big hand into her hair and pulled her mouth down to meet his, she let herself be kissed by Lukas McCoy.

5

GILLIAN FELL INTO THE KISS like it was the eye of a tornado. Everything around her was swirling, but there, in the center of it, there was only Lukas McCoy's mouth—steady and real. And it was made for kissing. Not too soft, not too firm—and oh so competent. Nothing clumsy going on here, she thought.

When he pulled his mouth away, she whispered, "The room is spinning."

"I know," he whispered back. His gaze never left hers while he rose to his knees. "Hold on to me." He gathered her into his arms and pressed her body firmly, surely, into his.

And still everything spun. Until she threw her good arm around his neck and put her mouth onto his.

Such comfort. Those big, strong arms holding her with such care. Such heat. His chest pressed against her breasts.

His hands moved down her back, clutched her waist, and lifted her with him as he got to his feet. He moved his hands down to her buttocks, then to her thighs, and settled her legs around his waist.

And all the while, he kissed her.

"Gillian," Lukas whispered roughly against her mouth before trailing his lips down her jaw. His skin felt like a fever when he buried his face in the crook of her neck. She thrust her hands into his hair while he kissed her neck and murmured words she couldn't hear against her skin.

Still holding her close, he walked over to one of the

chairs near the dressing room, swung her up into his arms, then lowered himself into it and settled her onto his lap. And then his mouth was on hers again and she sighed with the heaven of it. With the complete surprise of how it felt to be in Lukas McCoy's arms.

Lukas McCoy's arms? Gillian's eyes flew open.

She let out a squeal, pushed out of his embrace, jumped to her feet and stared down at him in horror. "This can never, ever happen again," she blurted out. "In fact, let's just forget it ever happened at all."

He was sitting there grinning at her. Swell, Gillian thought. Now he smiles.

"Might not be so easy to forget, princess."

Princess, again. Who knew the time would come when she'd prefer to be called *warden*?

"Well, make up your mind to forget it right now. And whatever you do, don't tell anyone about this. I mean—" Her mind flailed about, looking for some definitive reason that would keep either one of them from ever repeating the episode—incredible as it was. "I mean, it's—um—it's probably against the law!"

Against the law? Gillian knew she was really reaching on that one. Still—she didn't have that much ammunition to keep the whittler at bay and here he was, getting to his feet, that killer grin still on his face and coming toward her.

"I mean it, McCoy!" she yelled, holding out her hand like she was some kind of superhero trying to stop a train. "You better stop right there. After all—um—you're serving a sentence so anything—um—personal between us would be like a—like a guard fraternizing with a prisoner."

That stopped him. Took the steam right out of his locomotive. Killed the grin, too. "Fraternizing with a prisoner," he repeated in a flat voice. His mouth twisted but it in no way resembled a grin. "Sorry. I guess I forgot my place." He gave a little salute. "I'll get back to work right away, warden."

Gillian watched him head back to the display window and felt like a grade A bitch. But, darn it all, she had to do something to stop what was happening between them, didn't she?

Lukas went over to the window, picked up the carton, stuffed a couple of handfuls of lingerie into it, then started back toward her. His deep brown eyes sparkled dangerously. His full mouth was set into something between anger and a pout. Or maybe it was just his slightly turned-up, boyish nose that made her think that. Because when he spoke, he didn't sound at all like a pouting boy.

He thrust the box at her. "You better give me a different job to do, warden. Something that doesn't involve me getting my hands all full of silk and satin. We wouldn't want to get my mind on fraternizing again, would we?"

THE FOLLOWING MORNING, Lukas was riding shotgun in the Timber Bay Building and Restoration pickup while Danny drove. They were headed for work, but instead of pulling over at the hotel, Danny sped right by and aimed at the curb in front of the newspaper office down the block.

"There's my bride," he said with a grin.

Hannah was standing in front of the *Bay Bugle* office but she wasn't alone.

"Keep going!" Lukas snapped.

"What?"

"Just drive."

"What are you talking about? I'm gonna go by without saying hello?"

Lukas set his jaw as the truck rolled to a stop. Not more than three feet away, Hannah stood on the sidewalk, talking to Gillian.

Danny hopped out of the truck and sauntered over to Hannah, pulling her into a hug and a kiss. It was damn uncomfortable to witness with Gillian standing there. It made him think about last night. About Gillian in his arms. About her mouth under his. About her reaction to the whole damn thing. And here she was, wearing a black suit that made her look all sophisticated, with her sling covered in red silk. Too sophisticated for the likes of him. And hadn't she just about told him so last night? Oh, he'd been put in his place by the princess, all right. And he wouldn't forget it, either. He wasn't planning on stepping out of place again.

He pulled his whittling out of his pocket and got to work.

"Hey, Lukas! What about it?"

"What about what?" Lukas asked, keeping his eyes on the small wooden figure he was working on.

"Want to have coffee with the ladies over at Sweet Buns?"

"We got work to do," he said in a voice that he hoped would brook no argument. There was no way he was taking a coffee break with the warden. "Besides," he said as he glared at Gillian, "wouldn't that be fraternizing?"

Gillian tilted her head and fixed him with a cool, gray look. "The whittler has a wood chip on his shoulder."

"I think that might be a ball and chain you see, warden," Lukas said.

Gillian narrowed her eyes at him. "Watch it, McCoy, or I'll have you in prison stripes."

"Listen, princess—"

"Whoa!" Danny cried. "Time out, you two."

"Coffee is apparently a bad idea," said Hannah.

"Very bad," Gillian said, keeping her gaze fixed on Lukas.

"Yeah, it's bad enough we have to see each other at night," Lukas stated.

"Just see to it that you're not late again tonight, McCoy."

"Yes, sir, warden," Lukas answered, then turned to Danny. "You gonna stand there lookin' lovesick at your wife all day or are we gonna go to work?"

"I think I better go, darlin', before we have to break up a fistfight." Danny grabbed Hannah for a kiss goodbye, then hopped back into the truck. He shook his head at Lukas as he started the engine. "You two are acting like a couple of kids in the school yard who have a crush on each other but don't want anyone to know. Maybe Hannah was right about the legend."

"Aw, Danny, that's nuts," Lukas groused. Then he leaned forward and turned on the radio, fiddling with the knobs like he was looking for something that mattered. But all that mattered was that nobody, not Danny or anyone else, found out what went on in that dress shop last night. He'd never hear the end of it if they did. "You should see what she's planning on selling in that shop of hers. Stuff that must be making poor Aunt Clemintine restless in her wood box. You wait and see, she won't make it till Christmas. Yup," he said, settling on a country music station, "by New Year's the princess will be back in the city where she belongs. And we'll all be better off."

But that night at the shop, when the street was dark and quiet, and the air was cool enough for the old furnace to kick in every once in a while, they ended up in each other's arms again.

The kisses were hot, the breathing was loud and Lukas was about to make a stab at second base.

Gillian felt his big hands span her rib cage. She felt his thumbs brush the undersides of her breasts, slowly, patiently. She yearned for his hands to cover her. She wanted the warmth and the strength. She ached for it. Then, just as his palms started to cover her breasts, she saw reason.

"Wait a minute!" she cried, wiggling out of Lukas's arms and shoving a hand into her hair in exasperation. "We can't keep doing this!"

"If you're gonna pull that prisoner/warden thing on me again—"

"No—no!" She started to pace. "That was just me, stabbing in the dark, trying to come up with a way to make you keep your distance."

"It was?" Lukas asked.

She stopped her pacing and looked up at him. "Of course. I mean, we can't keep lunging at each other like this. We don't even *like* each other!"

He looked confused, then apparently thought it over. "You're right, we don't."

Gillian was aghast that he even had to consider it. "Well, no, of course we don't! Out there—" she made a sweeping gesture with her arm toward the front door "—we can't even be civil to each other. Then when night comes, and we're alone in the shop, and no one is around to see, we end up—" Her voice trailed off as she stared at his mouth. "We end up—um—"

"We end up doing this," he said. And then he took her into his arms and kissed her again.

Gillian was already kissing him back when she remembered that that was exactly what she didn't want to be doing. She pushed away from him again.

"You keep doing that, one of us is gonna end up with whiplash," Lukas grumbled.

"What we need is a diversion." Gillian looked around the shop. Her gaze landed on the two cartons of sweaters that needed to be tagged, folded and shelved. Not much of a substitute for lust. She still had to line the old display case with scented shelf paper, too. But somehow that prospect didn't quite live up to the idea of Lukas McCoy's mouth on hers, either. What she needed was substitute oral gratification. Something quick. Something satisfying.

"Sweet buns," she said out loud.

Lukas, who'd been bending down to rummage in his toolbox, looked over his shoulder. "You want me to keep my distance, princess, you better keep your opinions about my buns to yourself."

She crossed her arms and rolled her eyes. "Very funny, McCoy. I'm not speaking of your rear end," although, Gillian had to privately admit, it was pretty sweet, "but of your sister's cinnamon rolls. Did you bring any with you tonight?"

"Yeah," he answered, then took a bag out of his toolbox and handed it to her.

Gillian grabbed the bag. Saved. "I'm going to take a break."

"I'll come with."

"Nothing doing, McCoy. Distance is what we need."

She went upstairs, made a pot of coffee and warmed a bun in the microwave. Pirate hopped up onto the counter and scolded her with his unfeline rumblings so Gillian shared the frosting with him. When she went back downstairs, she took a mug with her—a peace offering for Lukas—and something to keep his hands busy.

He was in her workroom, looking at some sketches she'd tacked up on the bulletin board. When she came in, he turned around and took the mug she held out to him, watching her over the rim as he took his first sip.

"Did you do all these drawings?" he asked.

Gillian leaned against the doorframe and nodded.

"You thought this stuff up? Even the suit you were wearing this afternoon?"

"That's right," she said, waiting for the next remark that was sure to be cutting.

"You must have a lot going on in your head."

She searched his face, wondering if it was a trap. But he looked earnest. And handsome. And interested. Truly. "Something like that," she said.

"When I look at a piece of wood, I can sometimes envision what it should be. Not always right away. But if I feel it—" he said, making a grasping motion with one big hand "—hold it for a while—maybe live with it for a few days—"

She straightened from the doorway. "It comes to you," she finished for him. "It surfaces."

He grinned. "Yeah. Well put. It surfaces. I like that." He took another gulp of coffee. "It sounds like you know."

She nodded enthusiastically. "That white dress you like? I found the fabric first—absolutely fell in love the first time I touched it. I had to have it even though I wasn't sure what I was going to make. It wasn't until that night—the night of the—um—accident, that I saw what it should be. I knew its moment had come."

Lukas was shaking his head slowly. "Man. Nothing could be further apart than silk and wood, but—"

"But the creative process is the same," she offered.

He grinned. "Yeah, I guess it is."

"Well, we better get back to work," Gillian said.

"Hey—I was wondering. Did you find another branch for the window? 'Cause I might be able to help you out with that."

"Oh—really? Well, I started thinking that maybe you were right. Maybe the sight of all that underwear in the window would be too much for Timber Bay. I came up with another idea."

He seemed interested so she took him over to the alcove on the other side of the door and showed him how she'd hung a clothesline and used pastel clothespins to hang some of the lingerie. Under the clothesline she'd positioned old-fashioned laundry baskets that held the rest of the silky garments.

Lukas flicked a black thong with his finger. "I think I had a brief relationship with this one."

She laughed at that. And he laughed back. And then *he* was pushing back *her* hair for a change, letting his hand linger near her ear, letting his fingers trail over her cheek and down to her mouth. By now, of course, neither one of them was laughing.

He bent. She rose on tiptoe. And then they were kissing again. Long, slow, melting kisses—her good arm around his neck, her feet barely touching the floor because he held her so tight she was almost floating. And it seemed so easy when he cupped her bottom to wrap her legs around his waist again.

This time, the kisses deepened. Their tongues collided, danced, caressed. Their breathing quickened, the sound filling the silent shop. Gillian's heart beat frantically and the kisses went on and on until they were breathless, holding on to each other, nearly toppling, until Gillian's back hit the wall.

"Gillian," he said raggedly as he buried his face in her neck.

She arched back, raised her arm to tangle her hand in his hair, whispered his name. "Lukas."

Gillian knew her heart was pounding like mad, but suddenly it sounded absurdly loud. She opened her eyes. There was a shadow behind the sheer curtain covering the window in the front door. Someone was there, knocking.

"Lukas!" She struggled against his chest. "Please! Put me down!"

Lukas groaned. "Not another lecture."

"No! There's someone pounding on the front door!"

Lukas put her down so fast, he nearly dropped her. They straightened their clothes. They smoothed their hair. They both looked guilty as hell when they opened the door and Danny came in.

"Hey, buddy. Time's up," he said, pointing at his watch. "Sentence is over for the night."

Lukas just stared at him blankly.

"Did you forget? We're supposed to meet with Agnes Sheridan at the hotel. She wants to check out our progress."

"Oh! Right. I'll get my tools and be right with you."

Danny was looking from one of them to the other, a curious look on his face. Gillian decided to beat a retreat before he came up with any questions.

"Excuse me," she said. "I've—uh—got a phone call to make."

She went back to the workroom, shut the door behind her and leaned back against it. She looked at the dozens of bolts of fabric piled on shelves and wondered if any of them would make a good chastity belt. Because if this kept up, she was surely going to need one.

OUTSIDE, THE CRISP AIR STUNG Lukas's heated face. As they crossed the street, he wondered if Danny suspected anything. But how could he? Who would suspect that he and the princess could barely keep their hands off each other when they were alone? Lukas could hardly believe it himself.

"The Dragon Lady sure has a penchant for weird meeting times," Danny said. "When we got this job, it was a Saturday-night meeting in her parlor, remember?"

How could Lukas forget? It was right around the time that Hannah was tying Danny up in knots. Now they were headed for another late meeting with Agnes Sheridan—but it was Lukas who was a walking pretzel this time.

"Hey," Danny said, "you with me, buddy? You're acting a little strange."

Lukas tensed. He wasn't up for answering any prying questions—even from his best friend. "Just wondering what the old lady wants," he grumbled, "and why she couldn't ask for it during business hours."

"Ha! That one's easy. She can't stand to see us take a break."

Lukas got out his key but when he tried to fit it into the lock, the door creaked open. "Huh—she must be here already."

Danny looked up and down the street. "Funny. I don't see her Lincoln anywhere—or her chauffeur. Maybe she sent him home and plans on getting a ride from us in the truck."

The thought of Agnes Sheridan, wearing one of her ladylike hats and tapping her silver cane, riding shotgun in a pickup made Lukas relax at last. But when he saw who was waiting for them in the lobby, the tension shot back into his shoulders.

"You're late," Gavin Sheridan said as he pulled back the cuff of his coat and glanced at a watch that Lukas figured cost more than most people in Timber Bay paid for a car.

"We're not on the clock, Sheridan," Danny said.

"If you want to keep this job, then I suggest you be on time for meetings—no matter when they are."

"Our contract is with your grandmother," Danny pointed out.

Gavin Sheridan looked with disgust around the lobby. "Who has obviously seen better days," he drawled, "just like this place has."

"What's that supposed to mean?" Lukas demanded.

"I think he's saying that the old lady wouldn't have given us the job if she was in her right mind," Danny explained, his voice tight as a drum.

Lukas felt himself swell with anger. "There's nothing wrong with your grandmother's mind."

"Look, I'm not here to discuss family matters. I'm here to inspect your work. McCoy—you're obviously a man of talent. Your restorations are as good as work I've seen in Chicago. And lord knows this godforsaken town needs a better place for travelers to stay than that mom-and-pop place out on the highway. But I'm not convinced that you two are the ones to make it happen."

"Your grandmother is happy with our work so far."

"Of course she is, McCoy. She's a gullible old woman. She actually seems rather fond of you. Which leads me to believe that you've been kissing ass till your eyes water."

Lukas made a lunge toward Gavin, but Danny stepped in front of him and held him back. Lukas could have easily pushed Danny out of the way, but the look of warning in his partner's eyes stopped him. Danny was usually the hothead. If he was warning Lukas to behave, it would be wise to listen. He backed off.

Gavin smiled thinly. "Smart move. I don't think the two of you can afford a lawsuit—especially if I find a way to break your contract."

"You think Agnes Sheridan leaves loopholes?" Danny asked. "If you do, you're dumber than I remember."

"Loopholes?" Gavin shook his head. "Nothing that convenient, I'm sure. But I'm hoping I don't have to go so far as to have her declared incompetent."

"Incompetent?" Lukas scoffed. "You wouldn't have a leg to stand on."

"Think so? The woman is practically a recluse. She lives in the past and is bent on squandering the family's money and reputation trying to recreate something that can no longer possibly exist—and all as a trap to get me back here again." He cocked his head, the mild look on his face belying his words. "I don't know—sounds a little insane to me. And even crazier, she's hired you two to do it."

This time, it was Lukas who had to hold Danny back.

"Careful, boys. You may be looking for new jobs soon. Beating up the boss wouldn't look good on your resumé."

Lukas was tempted to just let Danny go when Gavin took his time walking to the door. But he genuinely liked Agnes Sheridan; he didn't want to let her down—and Timber Bay Building and Restoration couldn't afford to lose the hotel contract or the future business they hoped the job would bring them.

Gavin opened the door, then turned. "Have fun while you can," he said. "Because I have every intention of taking away your new toy."

As soon as the door closed behind him, Lukas let go of Danny.

"Man, I hate that guy," Danny said as he paced a short angry line up and down the lobby. "You should have let me rip his head off."

"Yeah, and then Hannah would have ripped off mine."

Danny laughed and Lukas saw the tension go out of him. "You're right. Hannah would definitely not approve."

Lukas paced over to the French doors that led to the ballroom and gazed up at the crown moldings. He was almost ready to start work on them. He wondered now if he was going to get the chance. "Hell. I knew when I saw Gavin last night that there was going to be trouble. I even said to Gillian—"

"Stop right there—you knew Sheridan was in town last night and you didn't tell me? How could you not have told me? We're still playing on the same side, right?"

"Jeez, Danny—of course. I just—well, I forgot."

"You forgot, huh?"

Danny studied Lukas until he felt like squirming. "Let's get out of here," he said. "I've got plenty of stuff to do at home." It wasn't a lie. But mostly Lukas wanted to get out of here before Danny started probing.

No such luck.

"Hang on, buddy. You're not going anywhere until you tell me what's going on with you."

"What do you mean?"

"I mean, what's got you so distracted that you forgot to tell me that Gavin Sheridan was back in town?"

Lukas scowled. "A guy can't forget something?"

"Sure, buddy. Especially if a woman is what's taking up his mind. And I don't blame you—Gillian Caine is a hell of a woman. But we have to stay focused—more than ever now that we know Gavin is planning to get this contract away from us."

"Look—the only woman in my life right now is Agnes Sheridan. So if you don't mind, I'm going home to get a good night's sleep so I can put in a day's work tomorrow that'll make Gavin Sheridan eat his words."

Danny smiled and slapped Lukas on the back. "Good. Then we're definitely still playing for the same side."

They locked up the hotel and went to their respective trucks but, long after Danny's taillights had disappeared, Lukas still sat in his, staring across the street at the dress shop.

The lights were still on. She was somewhere behind those filmy panels. The knowledge made his body stir. Maybe he should go over there and finish what had started when Danny had interrupted them.

But then what? It didn't really matter what happened between them behind those gauzy curtains every night. Because once the sun was up, it became as much of a dead end as where Sheridan Road met the Sheridan Estate.

And that brought Gavin Sheridan to mind again. He was undoubtedly just the kind of man that Gillian Caine would be happy to be seen in public with. She wouldn't be hiding behind a curtain with him, that's for sure. Why, she'd practically been drooling last night. And that wave—

Danny was right. Lukas needed to keep his wits about him. And there was no denying that Gillian Caine drove him just about witless.

A slight, curvy shadow wavered behind the pastel silk and then the lights of Glad Rags went out. Lukas rolled down the window and took a deep breath of the cold night air. Not as good as a cold shower, but it would have to do. It'd be a relief when his sentence was over and he never had to step foot in that shop again.

He started the truck engine and pulled away from the curb, keeping the window down all the way home.

LUKAS PUSHED OPEN the door to Belway's Burgers and Brews and waited for his eyes to adjust to the gloom. He wasn't much for sitting in taverns, but Danny had a standing lunch date with Hannah on Thursdays so Lukas had gotten into the habit of walking over to Belway's for a burger. As far as he was concerned, they were the best in town. A bunch of the old high-school crowd, guys from the football team mostly, were hanging out at the far end of the bar. They called out to him, but he just waved and slid onto a stool at the other end.

"Hi there, Lukas," Ina Belway said from behind the bar. "The usual?"

"Yup, Ina. The usual."

Ina put in his order then came over and set a mug of beer in front of him. "So how's things over at the dress shop?" she asked.

Lukas shot a quick look over at the aging jocks down the bar. "Hey," he said quietly, "keep it down. Last thing I need is for that bunch over there to start ribbing me about working in a dress shop."

Ina lowered her voice and leaned her elbows on the bar. "Well, you aren't exactly working in a dress shop. You're working *on* one."

"Huh. You think that bunch is gonna care about the difference?"

Ina shrugged. "I'd think you'd be more worried about getting ribbed about the legend."

Lukas nearly choked on his beer. He wiped his mouth on his sleeve, then said, "Not you, too, Ina." Ina was in her late fifties, a widow. She was weathered and blunt and he never saw her in anything but a T-shirt advertising some kind of beer and a pair of jeans. In short, she wasn't the type, in Lukas's opinion, to believe in fantasy.

"Well, when Kate said—"

Kate. Swell. Danny's mother never failed to speak her mind, no matter how outrageous. So now he had Hannah, Molly, Kate and Ina talking about him and Gillian. He should probably expect a call from his mother any day now.

"Look, Ina, the legend is not in play here. The tunnel had nothing to do with bringing me and Gillian Caine together."

"But Kate said—"

Luckily, someone in the kitchen called that his burger was up and Ina went to fetch it. She served him, then had to go refill drink orders for the jocks who were honking away about something that they found funny. Probably the usual locker room jokes. Or at least he hoped. But when Ina turned and looked at him, then bent her head low toward the quarterback from the class of '89 to say something private, Lukas started to wish he'd gotten his burger to go. He decided to wolf it down and get out of here. He was getting some bills out of his wallet when someone yelled, "Hey, McCoy! I hear you got a ball and chain and you ain't even married!"

"Yeah, Lukas," someone else hollered, "I hope she ain't makin' you try on the dresses so she can pin up the hems!" There was much guffawing after that one.

"Seems to me that you know too much about sewing there, buddy," Lukas shot back. This time the laughter wasn't at his expense. He yelled a goodbye to Ina and left without finishing his beer.

Out on the sidewalk, he stood for a moment until his eyes adjusted to the sunlight again. It was the kind of sunny October day when the temperature defied the season. But there was no mistaking it was autumn. There were signs of the coming Harvest Festival everywhere. Out in front of Nelson's Market, the grocery store across Ludington Avenue from Belway's, a life-size scarecrow stood guard over a large wooden crate of pumpkins for sale. A big sign in the window, decorated with colored leaves cut out of construction paper and silhouettes of witches flying on their brooms, promised a sidewalk sale of pumpkin cookies, pies and muffins along with hot apple cider for the festival at the end of next week.

This was one of Lukas's favorite times of the year but as he crossed the street and walked through the automatic door at Nelson's, he was in a foul mood. And it wasn't only because of the ribbing he'd just gotten.

He couldn't find Tiger. It was why he was in Nelson's— to buy cat food. He figured if he put a few open cans out on the terrace behind the hotel, the cat might show up. Lukas missed the old tom. The other thing on his mind was Danny. Lukas had never kept anything from him before. Not telling Danny about the things that happened with Gillian in that shop at night almost felt like lying. He knew that Danny sensed something. And maybe last night he would have gotten around to the subject—if Gavin Sheridan hadn't showed up with all that nonsense about declaring the Dragon Lady incompetent.

But what could Lukas have told Danny, anyway? The whole thing made no sense. He and Gillian couldn't get a civil word out to each other in public, but after nightfall, with the two of them alone and all that silk and lace around—

He rounded the corner of the pet-food aisle and there she was—smack dab in front of the canned cat food. Gillian, in another dress that made her look like something good enough to eat. He swung around before she saw him and headed down the next row—moseying along, not paying much attention to anything, just killing time until the cat food section was princess-free. When he was halfway down the aisle, Gillian came around the corner. She hesitated when she saw him. Silhouetted there, with the fresh meat case behind her, she looked better than she had in his dreams last night. The rest of the grocery store just sort of evaporated as they stared at each other.

"Hey, Lukas, how's that hotel job coming along?"

Lukas jumped at the sound of Gertie Hartlet's smoke-roughened voice. He grabbed the first product off the shelf beside him and acted like he'd been too engrossed in reading the label to hear her.

Gertie slapped him on the back. "You're a little young to be going deaf, aren't you, Lukas?" She peered at what he was holding in his hands. "Something we don't know about you, boy?" she asked.

Lukas's head shot up. "What's that mean?"

Gertie nodded at Lukas's hand. "If you get a plus sign, boy, you're gonna make history." She started to laugh but ended up coughing.

Lukas looked down. In his hands was a pregnancy test. He shoved it back on the shelf in a hurry and looked around. No one was watching—not even Gillian. She'd disappeared from the end of the aisle. Leaving Gertie digging for something in her purse, Lukas headed for the meat case. He wasn't sure why, but suddenly carrying around a thick, raw steak seemed like a good idea. He chose a manly sirloin then went back to the pet food aisle and grabbed a couple of cans and headed for the checkout lanes.

The lines were long in every lane except express. Lukas headed that way, then hesitated when he saw that Gillian Caine was the last one in line. Afraid that it would raise questions if anyone saw him turn and get into one of the long queues with his four items, Lukas reluctantly got in line behind her.

Gillian knew he was there before she even turned around. She could smell him—wood shavings, pine. She'd seen him scurry out of the aisle she was in earlier and she wanted him to know that she knew he was avoiding her. "You needn't worry that I'll force you to speak to me. It's obvious that you're trying to avoid me."

"Shh. Don't talk to me," he said out of the corner of his mouth.

She arched her brow. "If that's your idea of ventriloquy, I advise you to keep your day job."

"People are saying stuff about us—that's why I'm talking like this. I don't want to add fuel to the fire."

Gillian took a quick, anxious look around. There was a group of women by the bakery case near the front of the store. She thought she recognized some of them from the quilting club at the Church of the Holy Flock, including that loudmouth real estate agent. They were in some sort of hushed discussion. When one of them looked over at Gillian and Lukas, Gillian grabbed a magazine from the rack, held it up in front of her face and pretended to study the cover.

"What could anyone possibly be saying?" she hissed. "Have you been talking?"

Lukas grabbed a magazine and flipped it open. "Of course not," he said from behind it. "But I could tell that Danny was suspicious last night." It sounded a little lame but there was no way he was mentioning the legend.

"Well, no one could possibly know anything and no one's going to find out anything because it's never going to happen again."

"That's fine by me, princess. I'll keep my distance if you'll keep yours."

"Just what does that mean?"

"Well, I haven't been kissing myself, princess. You've been a little on the willing side."

Gillian gasped and forgot about holding the magazine up. There was an enhanced buzz from the direction of the church ladies. She jerked it up again.

"I am not *willing*, as you put it so charmingly. So don't count on it ever happening again. I have no intention of becoming the laughingstock of this town."

"What in blazes does that mean?"

"It means I won't have people talking behind my back about you being my court-ordered love slave or something."

"*Love slave?*" Lukas repeated loudly enough for the cashier to hear. The woman giggled.

Gillian sent her a withering look, returned the magazine to the rack and started to unload her cart. After she paid her bill and grabbed her bag of groceries, she turned around to look at Lukas. "Happy reading," she said with a nice, bright smile. Then she swished out the door.

Lukas frowned. What did she mean by happy reading? He put his cans of cat food down.

"You buying that magazine?" the cashier asked.

Lukas had forgotten he'd been holding it. "Uh—yeah," he said, and slapped it down on top of the cat food.

It was only then that he noticed it was a copy of *Cosmopolitan* and the biggest story, the one heralded in the boldest print, was: *How to Pick the Perfect Party Dress for the Holidays*.

"Lukas, you're beginning to worry me," Gertie Hartlet said from behind him.

The cashier started giggling again and Gertie started coughing again. By the time he paid for his groceries and got out of there, Lukas's face was more colorful than the pumpkins for sale out front.

6

By THE WEEKEND, there was still no sign of Tiger. The idea that he'd moved on made Lukas feel grumpy and under-appreciated. The darn cat had put away several dollars' worth of tuna sandwiches from Ludington's. Where was the appreciation?

He spent the weekend doing projects around the Victorian house he owned and was restoring. He'd decided it was time to tackle the kitchen—make the place more habitable. He was measuring the floor for ceramic tiles when Danny found him.

"Another busman's holiday, pal?"

"You got a better idea?"

"Yeah. Hannah and I are going for a drive in the country to pick apples. Why don't you grab a girl and come along?"

"You got a girl in mind?" Lukas asked suspiciously. Danny knew he hadn't had a date in nearly two years.

"Seems to me a girl like Gillian Caine might benefit from an autumn afternoon out in the country."

"Gillian Caine would benefit from a dunk in the bay. But I'm not the one who's going to give it to her."

Danny laughed. "Okay, then—come along with us anyway."

"And watch you two necking under an apple tree all afternoon? No, thanks." Just lately, being around the newly-weds made Lukas feel a little lonely—which made no damn sense at all. How could a man be lonely when he was with two of his very favorite people?

Danny leaned on the kitchen counter and crossed his arms, showing no sign of leaving for his afternoon in the country.

"Something else on your mind?" Lukas asked.

"I heard a rumor. Might be nothing—but on top of our recent run-in with Gavin Sheridan, it's troubling me."

Lukas tossed the tape aside and got to his feet. "Well—spill it," he said impatiently.

"Uncle Tuffy heard that one of those women that Sheridan brought to town with him works for a big hotel chain."

Lukas ran his hand through his hair. "Damn. Where'd he hear it?"

Danny shrugged. "He can't remember. But you know what Tuffy's day is like. He makes regular stops at the drugstore, the tavern, the barber shop—"

Tuffy was Danny's old bachelor uncle. He was as simple as they came but, as far as Lukas knew, he never made anything up. He did get things wrong sometimes, though. "So what do you think?"

Danny shrugged again. "I don't see Agnes Sheridan selling out to a chain. So maybe Gavin wants her declared incompetent for more reasons than just getting rid of us."

"I was thinking the same thing. It puts a whole new spin on things."

"Indeed it does," Danny agreed. "I'm no big fan of Agnes Sheridan's, but I'm hoping this is one of those times that Uncle Tuffy got it wrong."

Lukas didn't share Danny's view of the old lady. He liked her more each time he saw her. "I don't like the sound of this at all," he muttered. "What do you think we should do, Danny?"

"Not much we can do but wait and see."

After Danny left, Lukas found that he'd lost his enthusiasm for ceramic tile. He went out the back door, crossed the porch and went down the steps and over to the garage that he and Danny had converted into Timber Bay Building and Restoration. Once a carriage house, the place was huge. They'd made a small office just inside the side door. A workroom and a storage area took up the rest of the space.

The place welcomed him warmly with the scent of wood and leather. The carriage house felt like more of a home to him than the main house did. Lukas had always figured that the discrepancy would take care of itself as he worked on the house and made it his own—and found a woman to make his own, as well. But it wasn't happening. Not the house or the woman.

He walked over to the window in the office area. It gave a good view of the house. He wondered if Gillian Caine could live in a place like it.

Gillian Caine? Lukas snorted and shook his head at himself. What was he thinking? Didn't he have bigger problems to occupy his mind? Like losing that hotel contract—which would make measuring for kitchen tiles pretty much a waste of time. And the idea that the place could be sold to a chain. Like a chain would care if those crown moldings in the ballroom were exact replicas. The bottom line is what would matter. Yeah, he definitely had bigger problems to think about.

Besides, Gillian had made it clear that it was hands-off. And for the last few nights, ever since they ran into each other at Nelson's, he'd kept his hands off. He'd been relieved that she'd stayed back in the workroom with the door shut most of the time. Once in a while she'd come out to check on him or tell him what she wanted done, but then she'd go behind that door again.

But even though she'd been out of sight for the most part, it'd been hellish keeping his mind off of her amid all that satin and lace, amid dresses like he'd seen on her body, amid the scent of her that seemed to be everywhere.

He hoped the weekend off would clear his head, but by Monday evening, Lukas was feeling even more out of sorts.

"Lukas, you're acting like a cat that was left out in the rain." Molly put a bag of cinnamon buns down in front of him.

Lukas, hunched over a cup of coffee, said, "It's the job, that's all. Gavin Sheridan is going to be trouble—just like he always is."

"Is there any truth to the rumor?"

Lukas looked up sharply. "So you've heard it, too?"

"Tuffy said he'd heard something about the place being sold to a chain. Then, yesterday, these two women came in here. They were all dressed up in power suits and one of them had a portfolio with the name Brunswick on it."

"Brunswick Hotels?"

Molly shrugged. "Didn't say hotel but considering the rumor, it's a safe bet, I think."

"What were they like?"

"Snooty." Molly grinned. "Until they tasted the coffee, that is. They each bought a couple of pounds of the house blend. Paid with a gold card. They said they wanted to take it back to Chicago with them."

"Did they say when they were heading back?"

"I got the impression they were leaving this morning— with Gavin. That's a good sign, right?" Molly asked.

Lukas shrugged. "I don't know. I'm still uneasy about what Sheridan said about his grandmother. If Agnes Sheridan is incompetent, then I can't whittle."

"Exactly why you shouldn't worry about it. Gavin was just throwing his weight around. He's been doing it since he was in the first grade." Molly leaned over and rested her elbows on the counter. "I get the feeling something else is bothering you, brother of mine."

Lukas decided to try evasion. "Like possibly losing the biggest job the company has ever had isn't enough to bother me? It's a lot of money, sis."

"It'll be a loss, sure. But you've been through lean times before."

Her scrutiny was making Lukas itchy. As if he wasn't uptight enough already just at the thought that he was going to have to see *her* again that night.

"It's Gillian, isn't it?" Molly finally asked.

"Of course it's Gillian," he yelled.

His sister straightened and pumped her fist into the air. "Aha! I knew it! The legend is coming true again, isn't it?"

Lukas groaned. "Not you, too!"

"Well, when Hannah explained it to me, it made sense."

Lukas stood up and grabbed the white bag. "In case you've forgotten, sis, I'm serving a sentence over there at the dress shop. And I'm not enjoying being the big-city princess's slave one damn bit."

He started to move for the door when Molly said, "Her *love slave?*"

He whipped around. She had that same grin on her face that she'd had when she'd been a kid always teasing him, always following him around.

"Where did you hear that?" Lukas demanded.

Molly shrugged. "Word gets around."

"Well, the wrong word is getting around—and I'd appreciate it if you'd kindly let people know that."

"Sure enough, Lukas. Be happy to—"

Lukas opened the door.

"—if you let me borrow the latest copy of *Cosmo*."

Lukas swore and slammed the door shut behind him.

He strode across the street and burst into the back room at Glad Rags without bothering to knock. Gillian looked up from the sketch she was working on.

"My sister just made a crack about borrowing my copy of *Cosmo*," Lukas said.

"Excuse me?" Gillian asked.

"And she said something about a love slave, too. Have you been talking?"

Gillian threw down her pencil. "Are you kidding? I'm the one who asked you to keep it quiet, remember?"

Well, that was true, Lukas thought. That took some of the storm out of him. "Then how does she know?"

Gillian chewed her lower lip for a few seconds before answering. "That checkout clerk at the market? Maybe Molly knows her."

It made sense, thought Lukas. Damn—he should have questioned Molly instead of tearing over here to accuse Gillian. This wasn't like him. On the other hand, he'd never been in this situation before. Sentenced to work in a dress shop with a woman that could make him crazy—in more ways than one. "I don't want the whole damn town thinking I'm your love slave."

"You think I do? I'm a businesswoman, McCoy. I intend to be taken seriously in this town."

Lukas flicked a black ruffled cape hanging from a hook. "Then maybe you should stop putting ruffles on everything," he said.

She glowered at him. "You know, I heard that the Sheridan Hotel might be taken over by a chain. I sure hope so because it's probably the only way I'm going to get any fashion-savvy customers in this town."

"It figures you'd be happy about that. Tradition means nothing to someone like you."

"It's called progress, McCoy. This town could use some."

"This town doesn't need the kind of progress you're talking about. It doesn't need to lose itself to outsiders who shoulder their way in here and start changing things and trying to tell everyone what to do and how to do it."

"I get the feeling, McCoy, that you're not talking about the hotel. And as long as you think I'm trying to tell everyone what to do, allow me to tell you to get started cleaning that chandelier." She pointed at the ceiling. "And be careful. Those are real crystals."

Lukas looked up and groaned. There were hundreds of the little suckers and they were as dull as a worn hammer.

Fifteen minutes later he was up on a ladder, soapy water dripping down his arms, his big hands making a clumsy job of washing the small, ornate shards of glass. And if that wasn't punishment enough for arguing with the princess, from his perch he had a perfect view of her at work painting the dressing room.

Every time she bent to reload her paintbrush from the can at her feet, he could see the soft shadow of cleavage beneath her chambray work shirt. Every time she reached to paint high on the wall, he could see a couple of inches of bared midriff between her shirt and her jeans. Every time she squatted to wipe a spatter off the floor, he could see her thighs flex, see the denim draw tight over her bottom.

He tried not to look. But most of the time he failed. He'd been bellowing about being called her love slave yet here he was sneaking looks down her shirt and salivating over her backside. Less than half an hour ago they'd been disagreeing like politicians in a debate over something that was important to Lukas. Now he was starting to ache for her all over again.

Only four more nights of the tempting little warden. The Harvest Festival started Friday. Glad Rags would have its grand opening. After that, he'd be a free man. He looked around the shop. It looked terrific, there was no denying it. Lukas didn't know much about dress shops, but he knew that. But the clothes—no one in Timber Bay was going to buy them. Lukas still figured Gillian would be out of business—and out of town—before the New Year. And he'd be glad to see her go. Glad to see life get back to normal again.

Gillian turned her head and caught him watching. "Got something else on your mind, McCoy?" she asked.

"Uh—I was just—" His mind raced. He sure couldn't tell her what he'd really been thinking. "I was just admiring how well you—uh—paint," he finally blurted out. He cringed, knowing how lame that sounded.

Surprising him, she said, "I love to paint. Always have. It used to be a treat for me."

"A treat?" Lukas pictured the countless fence pickets he'd had to paint when he was growing up. Not one of them seemed like a treat.

She nodded. "I'm the only daughter in a family with four boys. My brothers are all great guys, but I hated being the only girl. None of them was expected to help with housework so I got stuck with all the inside chores while my brothers got to be out in the fresh air, painting the fence or the garage or doing yard work. Plus, I always had to wear their hand-me-downs."

Lukas watched her scrape paint off her brush and put the lid back on the can. "I always figured you for a spoiled rich kid."

She looked up at him in surprise. "Me? No way," she scoffed. "My dad is a proud member of the boilermakers' union."

Blue-collar background? Lukas never would have figured that one. "But you always wore all those fancy clothes."

Gillian wiped her paint-spattered hands on her work shirt. "Aunt Clemintine liked to spoil me. She thought it was terrible the way I was always in my brothers' old jeans and T-shirts. Whenever I'd visit, she'd make clothes for me. That's how I learned to sew." She had a sweet smile on her face and a wistful look in her big gray eyes. "Those hot summer days I spent in the back room with Aunt Clemintine were some of the happiest times I ever had in my life. She made me feel special."

She looked so appealing, standing there with paint on her nose and in her hair. She glanced up at him and then dipped her head, as if she were suddenly shy, and started fussing with the hair on a clunky old mannequin. He wondered if she was embarrassed about what she'd said. About what she'd let him see.

There was a clumsy silence, then she asked, "I know you have Molly, but do you have other brothers or sisters?"

He shook his head. "Just me and Molly."

"Are you close?" She started to push a mannequin toward the front of the shop.

"Oh, yeah. I mean we fight a lot and she drives me nuts sometimes—like when she asked to borrow my *Cosmo* tonight." Gillian started to laugh and Lukas found himself joining in. It was happening again. They were getting along. Was Hannah right? Was it the tunnel?

He leaned against the ladder and watched her. She had a determined little frown on her face, but the mannequin, all joints and seams, wasn't cooperating.

"Gillian, maybe you better let me help you with that," he said as he started down the ladder.

"Thanks. I think this thing was built before plastic was invented. It weighs a ton."

"Where are you going with it? The window?"

Gillian swung around to answer him and one of the mannequin's arms came flying off and hit Lukas in the chest.

"Oh, my gosh! Are you all right?" Gillian cried. Instinctively, she bent toward him and knocked Lukas's head with the mannequin's.

"*Umpf!*" he said, then staggered back and landed with a thud on one of the slipper chairs near the dressing room. His legs were sprawled in front of him, his head thrown back, his eyes shut.

Gillian let go of the rest of the mannequin and rushed over to peer into Lukas's face. "Lukas! Are you all right? Lukas! Talk to me!"

He opened one eye. "If we keep doing this to each other, princess, neither of us is going to live to see the Harvest Festival."

She slapped him on the arm. "You scared me!"

"*I* scared *you?* I thought I was supposed to be the dangerous one around here."

Oh, he was dangerous, all right. Sprawled in that chair, his hair mussed, his eyes laughing, his dimples almost blinding her, he was about as dangerous as it got. Time for a little bravado. "I think I still owe you a bruise or two, McCoy," she said as she started to turn away.

He caught her hand and pulled her into his lap.

"Hey!" she squealed, squirming to get free.

"Just thought I'd make it easier for you to bruise me, princess."

She arched a brow. "Do I have to give my fraternization lecture again?"

"Go ahead. I love it when you get all legal."

"Then let me remind you, inmate McCoy, it's now ten o'clock and your sentence is over for the night."

"I don't mind serving a little extra time, warden."

"Oh, but I wouldn't dream of inflicting any cruel and unusual punishment on the prisoner."

"Too late." His gaze moved over her face, then came to rest on her mouth. "Not being able to kiss you is already cruel and unusual punishment."

She went still. "Oh," she said. "Well, I guess we can't have that, can we?"

His dark eyes glittered. "Then you won't file a complaint with the court if I do this?" he asked. And then he lowered his head and took her mouth with his.

Illegal. That's what his mouth should be declared. It

was far more risky than driving at eighty miles an hour. She had that spinning sensation again. It was so easy to fall with the touch of his mouth. Too easy.

She pulled away.

"Gillian?" he whispered

Looking up at him, she saw the question in his eyes. She didn't know the answer—not yet—so she buried her face in his chest and felt the warm, soft flannel under her cheek.

She loved being in his arms. And what was the harm? It was only for here—for now. In four days his sentence would be over. Outside the shop, they couldn't get along. So there was no future between them to worry about. This was definitely a no-commitment-hunk opportunity. A girl didn't get offered that very often. In fact, Gillian had never been offered it before.

"Gillian?" he said again as he lifted her chin with his fingers. He grinned. "God, you look pretty with that paint on your nose."

She decided to take the offer.

"Shut up and kiss me, whittler."

And he did. And she spun. There was nothing to do but hang on and try to keep her head. But when his hand moved up her rib cage and covered her breast she lost control. Her nipple hardened immediately, shamelessly. He took advantage of it, coaxed it, brushed it until she had to pull her mouth away from his to gasp. Burying his mouth in her neck, he stroked and teased her breast. Her body bucked and she cried out. He groaned and took her mouth again while he worked on the buttons of her shirt, then slipped his big, warm hand inside her bra. When his fingers closed on her bare nipple she cried out into his mouth.

Lukas had never known anything like it. Her response made him crazy. It made him want more.

She was like forbidden fruit in his hands. Ripe, fragrant, sweet. He had to taste. He pulled his mouth from hers, then gently lowered the lacy cup of her bra until he'd freed her nipple, then he bent his head and took it into his mouth.

She moaned and writhed and bucked again. The sounds she made were incredible. Earthy. Wild. He had to hear her when she came. *He had to.*

He moved his hand down her body and cupped her between her thighs, pressing the heel of his palm into her. She moved wildly against his palm even as she said, "No, Lukas—don't—"

He raised his mouth from her breast and looked down at her. "Yes," he said. She started to protest again but he covered her mouth with his once more. He felt the surrender almost immediately. He moved his palm on her, knowing, somehow, exactly how to touch her. When she came, he pulled his mouth away so he could hear her, so he could watch her. When it was over, she went limp in his arms.

He gathered her up and she buried her face in his chest again. "That was the most beautiful thing I've ever seen," he whispered into her hair.

She peered up at him—shy and sweet. "I've never—I mean—not like that—it was just so—"

He palmed her face and drew it up to his. "It was just so beautiful," he said, and then he kissed her. When he pulled away, she had a little smile on her face.

"Your turn now," she said softly. "I mean—if you want me to."

Oh, he wanted her to. Lukas breathed a sigh of relief and resettled her on his lap so she could reach his zipper. He'd been hard before but he grew harder than ever as she eased the zipper of his jeans down and put her hand on him through his boxers. She stroked him and he threw his head back with the sharp pleasure of it. He had a feeling this was going to be over in an embarrassingly short time.

"You like?" he heard her whisper.

He looked down at her. At those big gray eyes looking

up at him. She wasn't the princess at all. Not tonight. To-night she was the girl next door. And she was his.

He bent his head until he was almost touching her lips with his. "More," he said, and then he put his mouth on hers. And all the while she gave him sweet release, he kissed her.

GILLIAN PICKED UP a magazine in the waiting room of the outpatient clinic of Timber Bay Memorial Hospital and flipped through it for a few seconds before tossing it back on the table. She looked at her watch again. One more hour and she would be with Lukas.

That is, if she ever got in to see the doctor.

This had to have been one of the longest days she'd ever lived through, waiting for the night. After last eve-ning, she couldn't get Lukas out of her mind. His mouth. His hands.

What would happen tonight? She grinned and felt a tiny shiver run down her spine. Anything could happen. And best of all, she didn't even have to worry if Lukas liked her or not. She already knew he didn't. And she didn't like him, either. It was lust, pure and simple.

Ah, simple. That's exactly what she needed after the Machiavellian manipulations of Ryan. A few more nights and Lukas would be just a memory. But she planned to make the most of those hours.

"Miss Caine?"

Gillian jumped. "Uh—yes?"

"Dr. Olsen will see you now."

The doctor was already in the examining room. She an-swered his questions and then hopped up onto the table to be checked out. He removed the sling then moved Gilli-an's arm up and down, back and forth, around and around.

"No pain?" he asked.

She cheerfully shook her head. "None."

"Excellent. Then I don't think we need this anymore." He picked up the sling and tossed it onto a cabinet.

"Don't need it?" Gillian asked as she looked at it lying all crumpled and alone.

"Nope. Just don't lift anything heavy for a few days and you should be fine."

"You mean—" Gillian gulped "—I can use my arm again?"

Dr. Olsen gave her a puzzled look. "That's what I mean. You sound disappointed. Last time I saw you, you couldn't wait to get the sling off."

"Oh—no." She smiled weakly. "No, of course I'm not disappointed. It'll be great to have two arms again." Except it meant she'd no longer have Lukas's arms around to help her.

Or to hold her.

Gillian jumped down from the examining table, thanked the doctor, and started through the maze of corridors from the outpatient clinic to the hospital lobby. Along the way she told herself not to be foolish. She didn't want Lukas McCoy's arms holding her—or helping her for that matter. After all, she'd taken a vow of independence, hadn't she? When she'd come to Timber Bay, she'd intended to do it all herself. The accident had merely derailed her for a short time. Now she could go back to her original plan—becoming a success without help from a man. If only she'd known that last night was their last night together.

"Oh, really, Gillian?" she muttered to herself. "And what would you have done if you'd known?"

No, it was really better this way. Last night had been wild and erotic—further than Gillian would have ever gone with a man she didn't have a real relationship with. So it was just as well that her arm had healed earlier than

expected before—well—before even more happened between them. As it surely would have. Oh, yes, this was definitely better.

Then why did she feel so inordinately sad at the thought
of setting the prisoner free?

The hospital lobby was still bustling despite the hour.
Gillian glanced at her watch. She'd still have time to make
it home and pull herself together before Lukas arrived.
She quickened her pace and was nearly through the lobby
when someone asked, "Aren't you the girl who sued Lukas
McCoy?"

Gillian stopped short, steam quickly building in her
head. She was in no mood for this. She swung around. An
elderly woman stood there, looking up at her through the
veil of a very chic little hat that was perched on her immac-
ulately coiffed white hair.

"Yes!" Gillian said. "I am the girl who sued Lukas
McCoy! But if you don't mind, it's none of your business.
Lukas McCoy is a big boy—a very big boy—and I'm sure
he can take care of himself just fine!"

The small woman's impressively erect shoulders stiff-
ened perceptively. Her eyes flashed like sparks on steel. "I
see you didn't inherit your aunt's manners, young
woman. I was willing to try your shop on the basis that
you were Clementine's niece. Such a dear woman. But I
don't like your attitude, miss." She rapped her silver-
tipped cane smartly on the floor. "I patronized your aunt's
shop almost exclusively. But, based on what I've seen so
far," she gave Gillian a once-over that was worthy of a
Manhattan matron, "I'm afraid I see shopping trips to
Chicago in my future. Good day, miss." She walked away
grumbling something about hoping a legend didn't come
true this time.

"Wait—Mrs.—uh—"

The woman kept walking. Gillian rushed up to the reception desk. "That woman—the one with the cane," she said, nodding toward the door. "Who is she?"

"Her?" the receptionist asked. "Why, that's Agnes Sheridan."

"Sheridan?" Gillian grimaced. "You mean as in the Sheridan Hotel?"

The nurse nodded. "The richest woman in town."

LUKAS RAN DOWN THE STAIRS, still rubbing his hair dry with a bath towel. He'd hurried home after working at the hotel all day so he'd have a chance to shower and change before seeing Gillian.

Down in the dining room, he tossed the towel on the old door stretched across two sawhorses that served as a catchall and work table, grabbed his jacket off the floor, and headed out the door.

The porch was scattered with leaves and next to the front door were pumpkins that his mom had brought over from her garden. Danny's niece had made him a couple of construction-paper ghosts that he had taped to the front window. He had little furniture, the kitchen was still torn up and he was living alone, but on the outside the place already looked like a home.

Lukas had bought the Victorian five years ago when he was twenty-five. At the time, most of his high school buddies were still spending their time and money on fast cars and nights out on the town. They'd all thought he was nuts for wanting to saddle himself with a house before he even had a wife, but Lukas didn't want to wait any longer. He'd always wanted a wife, kids and a house. He hadn't found the wife yet. But he knew he'd found the house as soon as it went on the market.

He'd fixed up the outside first, repairing the wood siding where it was needed, replacing the rotted sections of gingerbread and other trim with pieces he'd made himself.

Then he'd painted it rose and blue and green, in the style of the Painted Ladies he'd once seen in a magazine article on San Francisco.

He slid into the truck, smiling at the thought of the cargo in back. That afternoon, he'd gotten a huge branch from a birch tree that a neighbor had cut down. He planned to give it to Gillian to replace the one he'd fallen on. He could just imagine her smile when he gave it to her. Before he started the truck, he looked back at his house as he always did. Only this time, he saw Gillian Caine standing in the doorway.

He shook his head. "Don't be an idiot, Lukas," he muttered as he started the truck and pulled away from the curb. This thing with Gillian Caine had boundaries instead of a future. A few more nights, that was all. Meanwhile, he was darn glad it was October, when the nights were long.

But could they ever be long enough? All day he'd kept hearing the sounds she made when he touched her. He kept remembering how she felt under his hands. How she tasted on his tongue. In fact, the only time he wasn't remembering those things was when he was too busy remembering the feel of her hand on him and her sweet kisses as she brought him to a raging release. Love slave? Heck, he'd gladly be her love slave.

He groaned when he had to stop for a light. While he waited for the green, he wondered what would happen tonight. Would they talk? He hoped so. He was still knocked out that she came from a blue-collar family, and still intrigued at the way she withdrew after she'd let him see inside of her a little. Maybe this time they'd touch and kiss and—well— He felt heat spreading up his body and looked at the car next to him, hoping it wouldn't be anyone he knew. It wasn't. The light changed and he drove through the intersection thinking that maybe they'd talk *afterwards* tonight. While he held her.

His heart raced and he stepped on the gas, positive that no prisoner before him was ever in such a hurry to see the warden.

Gillian met him at the door. But not the Gillian of last night. Or any of the nights before. It was the big-city princess, all decked out in her finery, who stood there.

She looked cool, beautiful and unattainable in a dress he hadn't seen before. It was the same silver color as the pantsuit she'd worn that first day—sophisticated and cold as steel.

"Is something the matter?" he asked.

"Quite the contrary," she said. "Everything is terrific. See?" She held up her arm. "No sling. All better. You're a free man, Lukas McCoy. You've paid your debt to society."

She started to close the door and he said, "But—" but then his mouth filled with dust, just like it always used to around the princess.

"Was there something else?" she asked coolly. "If not, I have things to do."

Hell with the desert. Her attitude put the spit back into his mouth. "I was right. Cats don't change their stripes, do they?" he asked, thinking it was the same with Tiger. He'd gone back to wherever he came from, too.

"Excuse me?" the princess asked, her chin tilted high enough to put her nose in the air.

He made himself laugh. "Good luck, princess," he said. "You're going to need it." Then he turned around and walked away.

When Lukas reached the truck he looked in disgust at his precious cargo. Dead wood. Huh. "Nice gift, McCoy," he muttered, thanking whatever made him leave it in the car. Getting royally dismissed was one thing, but getting dismissed while carrying a gift of dead wood was another thing entirely.

Imagine what they'd make of that down at Belway's tavern.

Upstairs, Gillian sat in Aunt Clemintine's dark living room and watched him drive away. She sniffed and Pirate walked over and rubbed against her leg. "Why didn't I invite him in for one more night?" she asked the cat. Pirate sat down and looked up at her. "Why didn't I just keep the damn sling on and pretend to still be wounded?" Pirate gave her a disdainful look from half-lowered lids. She knew the cat was right. It was better this way. Pretending would have gotten her a few more nights with the whittler—and a few more miles further down the road to regret. "He might have at least protested," Gillian complained. Pirate closed his eyes completely on that one. And rightly so. Gillian had known very well that if she dressed like the princess he couldn't stand, he wouldn't protest. Which was exactly why she'd done it.

She stood up. "Good," she told Pirate. "My plan worked. It's over." She went into the bedroom and changed into jeans and a flannel shirt. The Harvest Festival and Glad Rags's grand opening were only three days away.

Back down in the shop, she couldn't seem to get busy. The place felt lonely without Lukas. They'd spent over a week together and he'd left his mark. Big man. Big mark.

"Ninny," she scoffed. He wouldn't have spent time with her at all if he hadn't been court-ordered to, for pity's sake! She should be dancing on the ceiling that things hadn't gone any further than they had with McCoy. Besides, she had bigger problems to worry about. Like the fact that she'd alienated the richest woman in town.

Gillian looked at all the sketches she'd tacked up on the bulletin board. All the clothes that she might never have a chance to make. True, if a big hotel chain bought the Sheridan Hotel it would mean publicity that could give the area a much-needed jolt of tourism, which would translate to sales for Gillian. But having the patronage of a woman like Agnes Sheridan would definitely have been a coup. Oh, the old lady wouldn't have bought anything from the *Urban Flannel* collection or the *Pastel-Metallic* collection. But Gillian was a designer. And Agnes Sheridan could afford to commission custom designs. That was one fence she was definitely going to have to try to mend. But first she had to get a certain whittler off her mind.

She grabbed a bolt of pale pink wool and got to work.

7

GILLIAN GLANCED at the clock and her heart gave a lurch of
excitement. In two more hours Glad Rags would be offi-
cially open. Tradition held that the shops and restaurants
on Sheridan Road stayed closed until five o'clock on the
opening night of the Harvest Festival. It gave the town a
chance to prepare and helped crank up the anticipation. All
day long city workers had been hanging little orange lights
in the trees that lined the Road and setting up booths for
games and food in the park on the bay. She had spent the
day putting the finishing touches on the Glad Rags display
window. Aunt Clemintine's old-fashioned mannequin was
wearing the white silk dress—the stardust dress—with the
long pink wool cape that Gillian had started making the
night she'd set Lukas McCoy free.

In lieu of the McCoy-busted silver tree and the clothesline idea, she'd put Clemintine's tall lingerie dresser in the
window with scarves, slips and accessories spilling out of
the open drawers. Atop the dresser was a huge bouquet of
yellow roses with a congratulation card signed by her parents attached to it. She had no idea that she was going to
miss them so much at this moment. She'd wanted to do
this all alone, but what she would have given to have them
with her today.

She dashed impatiently at a tear that had slipped down
her cheek. There was no time to get all sentimental. She still
had to go upstairs and get gorgeous for the grand opening.

At five o'clock sharp, the orange lights strung in the trees came on, the Chamber of Commerce started giving horse-drawn hayrides along Sheridan Road and Gillian drew open the sheer drapes in the window, turned on the pink neon sign and unlocked the front door of Glad Rags.

And then she waited.

But no one came.

A few adventurous souls stopped to look in the window, but most people went by like they thought they'd turn into a pillar of polyester if they looked. Lord knows what they thought would happen to them if they actually came in.

"Cowards," Gillian mumbled to herself as she looked at the clock. Almost time to close and not one customer. She wandered over to the little table between the slipper chairs where she'd placed a plate of miniature French pastries she'd had air expressed from a little bakery in the Village. She'd resisted them so far, but now her hand hovered over them as she decided which one to console herself with. The chocolate éclair looked the biggest. She plucked it off of Aunt Clemintine's tiered crystal plate and took a bite. The custard filling oozed out satisfyingly. She wandered around, licking her fingers, wondering if Aunt Clemintine had ever gone through this. But everyone in town had loved Aunt Clemintine. Unfortunately, that affection had not spilled over onto little Gillian. Oh, the adults had been nice enough. But if a customer had a kid in tow, generally the kid and Gillian would be busy making faces at each other while the adults discussed dress lengths. Those little girls she'd stuck her tongue out at were now her customer base.

"You were not the most popular girl in town, Gilly," she murmured as she licked the last of the éclair's frosting off her fingers. She'd been idiotic to think that that would have changed.

No. Not idiotic. Desperate. Desperate to get away from the mess she'd made of her life. Desperate to start fresh. Most of all, desperate not to move back to New Jersey to become *the girl who had failed*.

When the clock struck nine, Gillian closed the drapes, turned off the sign and locked the door. She took the plate of pastries upstairs, stowed them in the fridge and went to find Pirate. He was lying on her bed, licking a paw. She joined him, but managed to resist the urge to suck her thumb.

"What am I going to do, Pirate?" Pirate stopped licking a paw and looked bored but resolute. "Not one customer all night. They aren't going to give me a chance."

Pirate yawned.

"I know. Self-pity is boring. Believe me, I know. But what am I supposed to do?"

He got up, stretched, jumped off the bed and strutted out of the room.

The cat was right. Why should he listen? Nobody liked a crybaby. So instead of feeling sorry for herself, Gillian took off her flounced georgette dress, put on some nice worn flannel jammies, and sat down with a legal pad to try to plot how to turn tomorrow into a better day than today.

But Saturday wasn't any better than Friday. Still no customers, despite the fact that Gillian had come up with a terrific idea for a contest. She'd stayed up practically all night making a darling little rain cape out of some lavender vinyl she'd been carting around for years. Then, just as the first birds started chirping out in the alley behind the shop, she'd finished fashioning a wide-brimmed hat from purple-dotted vinyl. The adorable ensemble was going to be the prize in a drawing she would hold at the close of the day from entries customers filled out and dropped into the slot of a box she'd covered in Victorian wallpaper. There was a huge sign in the window to that effect. Unfortunately, the box was still empty and it was the middle of the afternoon.

Those French pastries were starting to look mighty good again.

LUKAS SAT at a table near the window at Sweet Buns, whittling. But he was also frequently checking out the people milling about Sheridan Road. So far, not one person had gone into Glad Rags.

"I hope you're planning on sweeping up those shavings yourself," his sister Molly said as she joined him. "What are you so busy watching, anyway?"

"Nothing," he muttered.

"Shame how nobody goes into Gillian's shop," Molly murmured.

"Don't they? I hadn't noticed." He tried to throw off the remark casually but Molly gave him a look like she knew better. "Guess your prediction was right," she said as she headed back to the kitchen.

Yeah, it looked as though his prediction had been right. So how come he didn't feel like running across the street to say *I told you so?* He should be celebrating the fact that the Princess might soon be out of his life forever. Instead he was feeling lousy through and through. Poor Gillian must be going through hell. She'd worked so hard. Been so hopeful. Couldn't at least one person go in and buy something? Even just try something on? He needed to do something. But what? It's not like he could go into Glad Rags himself and buy something.

But Molly could.

"Hey, Molly," he yelled as he went to find her. She was in the kitchen, taking a batch of scones out of the oven. "Do me a favor, huh?"

Molly laughed softly. "Yes, Lukas, you can have a warm scone."

"No, that's not what I want."

She looked at him. "Not like you to turn down food. What's on your mind?"

"I need you to go over to Glad Rags and buy yourself something."

Molly burst out laughing. "Right."

Lukas didn't get the joke. "Why not? What's wrong with helping out a fellow businesswoman?"

"Do you have any idea what she charges for her stuff? Even if I wanted to help her out, I couldn't afford to."

Lukas did some quick calculating in his head. There hadn't been any more gossip about the hotel and no word at all from Agnes Sheridan about canceling their contract—or anything else for that matter. His finances were in good shape. And he could always cut down on eating, if it came to that. "I'll pay for it," he said.

Molly's head came up at that. "*You'll* pay for it?"

"Yeah. Something wrong with a guy buying his sister a present? And since when do you balk at shopping, anyway?"

"Since I've got stuff to pack up for my booth over at the park, since I've got a daughter to take care of, and since I have coffee beans to grind."

"I'll do it."

"All of it?"

"Sure. Why not? I'll run over to the bank and get some money while you finish up your baking." Molly looked skeptical and was probably forming about fifty questions in her head. Dangerous questions. But Lukas was on fire with the idea. Now that he'd thought of it, he had to do it. "Do this, no questions asked, and I'll baby-sit every Sunday afternoon for a month."

"Done!" Molly said, and Lukas tore out of Sweet Buns and headed for the bank.

GILLIAN STROLLED past the plate of miniature pastries again. Okay, if she didn't get a customer in the next thirty—no, fifteen—minutes, she was going to eat one. She had her eye on a particular napoleon that was studded with sliced almonds.

Of course, she'd rather have the customer. Three in the afternoon and still not one customer despite the addition of the rain ensemble in the window next to the sign announcing the contest. You'd think it never rained in Timber Bay.

The bell above the front door jangled and Gillian actually felt a shiver run down her spine. A customer! Preparing herself to pounce and not let the woman out the door until she bought something, Gillian smiled jubilantly and turned around. A grizzled little man stood holding the doorknob.

"Oops!" he said with a lopsided grin. "Wrong place!" He started to leave then spied the plate of pastries. His eyes lit up like a jack-o-lantern.

"Please," Gillian said, "help yourself." She was pretty sure the elf wasn't in the market for a dress or pantsuit but every pastry he ate was a blessing to her hips.

The little man doffed his red-and-black plaid wool cap and shuffled happily over to the pastries, pocketed two and nibbled on the third while he wandered around the shop. Gillian held her breath when he started fingering things but when he saw the decorated box his face brightened in a gap-toothed grin. "What's this?"

Gillian explained the contest. He went over to the window to check out the prize.

"Well, ain't that pretty. Can I enter?"

"Well, sure. Of course." Gillian watched as the little man filled out an entry slip, printing Uncle Tuffy in big block letters, and stuffed it into the box, oblivious as to how lonely his entry was going to be.

After he left, she plopped down onto a slipper chair and

grabbed the napoleon that had been calling her name all afternoon. Just as she was shoving it into her mouth, the bell over the door jangled again and in walked Molly Jones. Not exactly the image she wanted to present to a customer but she jumped to her feet and tried to appear gracious despite the fact that her cheeks were stuffed with pastry cream.

"M-Molly," she said. "H-how—" she decided she had better swallow "—nice to see you again."

"So this is why you haven't been in for any of my cinnamon buns," Molly said as she took a pastry from the plate.

"I'm afraid not much could take the place of your sweet buns, Molly."

Molly laughed and popped the tiny pastry into her mouth. "Did Lukas satisfy you?" she asked after she'd swallowed.

Gillian's gaze shot to the slipper chair, the one Lukas had been sitting in when he—uh—had satisfied her. She gulped. "Um—well—"

"He can be pretty handy to have around," Molly added.

Oh, yes, Gillian thought. Extremely handy. But how did Molly—?

"The shop looks great, so I'm assuming everything worked out okay."

"Oh! The shop! Oh, yes—Lukas was great. He's very good with his hands," Gillian said, then blushed as soon as the words were out of her mouth. She decided to make herself busy straightening the lingerie but that only made her remember Lukas lying in the window, covered with panties and bras. And that only made her think of that first kiss. What luck. Her only customer all day and it had to be someone who made her think about Lukas again.

Not that she'd ever really stopped. She thought about him all the time. And one of the things she thought about was how easy it had been for him to just walk away. Sure, that had been the plan—and it was what she'd wanted. Absolutely. But that last night of his sentence—didn't he think of it at all? Because she could hardly stop thinking about it. Even now, with the whittler's sister just a few feet away, her body was heating in a most unprofessional way.

"No more McCoy-induced mishaps?"

"No, but I'm afraid I managed to inflict a few bruises on him."

"Hmm—yeah, you do seem to have left your mark on him."

Gillian's heart raced at those words and what they might mean. But she told herself not to be silly. "Your cinnamon buns have left a permanent mark on me, I'm afraid," she said as she patted her tummy.

"Oh, nonsense. My husband used to always say that all real women were zaftig."

"Excuse me?" Gillian asked, wondering if she'd just been insulted.

Molly laughed. "I didn't know what it meant either, until Billy told me. He was always using words I didn't understand. He was a teacher."

"Was?"

Molly nodded. "He died before Chloe was born."

"Oh—Molly, I'm so sorry."

"Thank you," she said simply. "Zaftig means having a full, shapely figure. Billy loved zaftig—even though he was one of those maddening people who could eat like a pig and still be thin as a pole."

"Billy sounds like he was a treasure."

"He was."

"Unlike Ryan the rat," Gillian murmured.

Molly laughed. "Ryan the rat? Not a pet, I take it?"

Gillian shook her head. "Not unless you consider a vulture a pet."

Molly settled down on one of the slipper chairs, and

picked up another pastry. "This sounds interesting. Are you going to tell me the rest of the story?"

Gillian hesitated for a moment, then decided she might as well spill her guts. Molly was the closest thing she had to a friend in Timber Bay and while she couldn't exactly discuss her labyrinth-like feelings for Lukas with his sister, she could tell her about the mess in Manhattan.

"Ryan is the reason I ended up in Timber Bay," she said as she sat down in the other slipper chair. "When I met him I was slaving away in the garment district in Manhattan, working on other people's designs. Ryan thought I had talent—or so he said. I had a little money saved and we went into business together and opened a boutique in Lower Manhattan around the same time—not coincidentally, as I found out later—we got engaged."

"You're engaged?"

"Was. Ryan turned out to be as phony as the diamond in the ring he gave me. When I found out he was cheating on me, I demanded cash for my share of the business. That's when I discovered that I didn't even own a share in it. The whole thing had been a hoax. He moved on to another designer and I came out here to start over."

"Rat might be too good a word for him," Molly said.

"I foolishly let him take care of the business side of things. When I found out the truth, I vowed I'd never let another man have any control over any part of my life ever again."

"When Lukas popped up out of the manhole and sprained your arm you must have felt like your plans were being derailed by a man again."

"Exactly! It's the reason I sued. I was too demoralized to take Ryan to court. I'm afraid I'd gotten some balls by the time Lukas sent me flying."

Molly laughed. "Far as I'm concerned, the big lug got what he deserved."

"I wish the rest of the town felt that way. I sued your brother so I could open Glad Rags in time for the Harvest Festival but it sure backfired on me."

"You think that's why you haven't gotten any business?"

"Well, isn't it? I mean, my clothes are good. I know they are."

"Your clothes are terrific—just not—well, it's hard to imagine Gertie Hartlet or Ina Belway wearing them."

Gillian groaned. "Now you sound like your brother. And you're both probably right, too. That's why when I heard the rumor that a national chain might buy the Sheridan Hotel, I got kind of excited. Something like that could attract tourists from Chicago and that would only be good for business."

"Hey, whatever you do," Molly warned, "don't tell Lukas that."

Gillian grimaced. "I'm afraid I already did. He was not pleased. Accused me of having something against tradition."

Molly laughed. "I can just imagine. Lukas is all for tradition. Don't get me wrong—that's one of the things I love about him. But the fact is, you're probably right. The kind of people that would come up here to stay in one of those luxury chains would love your shop." Molly grinned. "They'd love mine, too."

"Your sweet buns would become famous."

"Hmm—if that happened, I could franchise and then I'd be able to afford to hire you to make all my clothes."

Gillian grinned. "Now you're talking. We'd both become famous! Seriously, though—you really don't think the town is staying away because I took Lukas to court?"

Molly shook her head. "Small towns tend to be loyal about their own, but I really don't think that people hold it against you for suing my brother. If you think it's a possibility, though, then maybe if they knew the reason—"

Gillian jumped to her feet. "Absolutely not. A girl's got

to have some pride. You've got to promise me, Molly, here and now that you won't tell anyone what I just told you. Here," she picked up the plate of pastries, "swear on these that you'll keep my secret."

Molly raised her left hand and let her right palm hover over the plate. "I swear on pastry cream and chocolate frosting that the name Ryan the Rat shall never pass my lips."

Gillian laughed. Oh, she liked this sister of Lukas McCoy's. And she admired her. For Sweet Buns. For Chloe. For making a success of her life after going through the kind of thing that would emotionally cripple many women twice her age.

"You just earned yourself a ten-percent discount."

Molly jumped to her feet. "Then clear a path because I am about to shop!"

Gillian took care of some things in the back room while Molly looked around. "Find anything?" she asked Molly hopefully when she went back out front.

Molly held up a miniskirt and studied it dubiously. "Look," she said, "why don't we cut to the chase. Do you even have anything in this shop that is going to fit me?"

Gillian grinned. "Oh, Molly—as Aunt Clemintine would have said—you really are a breath of fresh air. I'm sure we can find something. What are you? A size ten?"

Molly grimaced. "Fourteen on a good day."

"Are you looking for something in particular?"

"Um—no. Just something different than my usual, maybe."

Gillian wished she'd listened to her mother about making clothes to fit women with breasts and bottoms. Zaftig, she thought with a smile. She couldn't wait to share the word with her mother. As it was, just about everything in the shop was going to be too snug for Molly's voluptuous body. And then she remembered the russet flounced georgette wrap dress. Gillian had been experimenting with clothing that was adjustable in size and its lines were very forgiving. It just might look wonderful on Molly.

"I have the perfect dress for you," Gillian said. "Be right back." She ran to the back room, transferred it from its cheap plastic hanger to a pink quilted one and headed back to the shop. "This color is going to be fabulous on you."

Molly took one look at it and shook her head. "No."

"No? But it's a fabulous dress!"

"Oh, Gillian, I know. It's positively beautiful. But remember Chloe's mud pies? This dress isn't exactly made for my lifestyle. The fabric looks so delicate. And those ruffles—"

"Just try it on," Gillian urged. "Can't hurt, right?"

Molly reluctantly took the dress and disappeared into the dressing room. Gillian found herself crossing her fingers that the dress would fit Molly. And not just because it might mean a sale. She loved her attitude about her body. She was busy mentally calculating how much more of a discount she could afford to offer when Molly came out of the dressing room.

"You look just incredible," Gillian said and meant it. The fabric draped Molly's body perfectly, accentuating the lush curves of her breasts and making her waist look small and feminine. The flounced ruffle at the deep V crossing of the neckline provided just enough cleavage to be provocative and the uneven hem showed off Molly's surprisingly shapely legs. "Shoes—you need shoes. And I've got just the pair. Be right back."

Gillian ran upstairs and dived into her closet, coming up with a vintage pair of sable suede toeless pumps with heels right out of a 1940s film noir. They turned out to fit Molly perfectly.

"You look stunning—just stunning," she said as Molly stood in front of the gilt-edged three-way mirror. "You simply must have that dress, Molly."

"Oh—I don't know—"

"If it's the money, you can pay me a little each week—"

"No, it's not that. It's just that—well, where would I wear it?"

Gillian could see Molly wanted it. How could she not? She looked like a goddess. "New Year's Eve?" she offered hopefully.

"I'm a widow with a toddler, Gillian. On New Year's Eve I'll be watching television in my bathrobe and eating pizza."

"Hey, it's almost two months away. Anything could happen." And didn't Gillian know the truth of that.

Molly grinned. "Okay. I'll take it."

Gillian rang up the sale and packed the dress between folds of pink tissue paper in a silver box. At the last minute, she added the pumps.

"Oh, I couldn't!" Molly protested.

"Tell you what, I'll trade you for a couple of cinnamon buns. I've been craving them for days."

Molly laughed, then surprised Gillian with a brief hug. After she left, Gillian stood in the window and watched her cross the street. It felt so damn good seeing that box under Molly's arm.

It was a start.

Unfortunately, she'd forgotten to have Molly fill out an entry slip for the contest. When closing time rolled around, there was still only one entry in the box and, much to Gillian's surprise, the entrant showed up in person for the drawing.

Uncle Tuffy was beaming when she pulled his name out of the box.

"Thank you, little lady," he said to her as she took the rain cape and hat out of the window and started to box it up, "but I think I'll just wear it."

"Excuse me?"

"I'm gonna wear it," he said. She started to open her mouth to tell him that it was meant for a woman, but he had already slung it over his shoulders. He looked so delighted that she saw no point in ruining it for him. So she helped him fix the brim of the hat at a rakish angle and off he went down the street, skipping so merrily that Gillian just had to laugh.

"Two satisfied customers," she said as she pulled the plug on the neon sign and prepared to close shop. One had already bought the only thing in the shop that would fit her and the other was the wrong sex. But what the heck, Gillian was going to count them as victories. She was, after all, in no position to be fussy.

When she got upstairs all she wanted was a hot shower and an old movie in the VCR. But the apartment felt lonely and Pirate had hidden away somewhere, no doubt in fear of another heart-to-heart. She strolled over to the window. Below her, the town was alive with the festival and suddenly Gillian wanted to go. And why shouldn't she? She'd sold a dress! Glad Rags was in business.

She pulled on jeans and a flannel shirt then topped it off with boots and a Navy pea coat. At the last minute, she tucked her hair into a knit cap. This was one night she wanted to blend in with the crowd. She intended to have the full Timber Bay experience. Check out the natives in their own environment. Maybe get some ideas on what sort of clothes would get them to cross Glad Rags' threshold.

She stuffed some cash into her jeans pocket and clattered down the stairs and out into the evening.

The wind was crisp and clean and it sent the tiny orange lights in the trees to dancing. She pulled her cap farther down on her ears and turned toward the park. There was the clip-clop of horses, and the laughter of children as a hay wagon passed by, and the scent of burning leaves and apples and—corn. Roasted. Gillian grinned, crossed the street and entered the park.

Kids in costumes lined up to bob for apples, take a shot at a pumpkin-shaped piñata, or play carnival games benefiting a local charity. There were booths selling hot cider and caramel apples and the Women of the Holy Flock had set one up that sold everything pumpkin—pies, muffins, cookies, butter. She bought a cup of hot cider and wrapped her hands around the warmth of it as she walked. The festival was like something out of a Normal Rockwell illustration. Only better, because it was real. And she was part of it. Well, not really, she thought as she sipped cider. But she would be.

If these people would let her.

MOLLY HANDED Chloe to Lukas. "Here," she said, "hold her while I buy a pumpkin pie."

"No problem. Come here, pumpkin," Lukas said. Chloe really was a pumpkin tonight, in a costume that Molly had ordered out of a catalog. He bounced the little girl up and down as he scanned the crowd for what felt like the hundredth time.

He kept telling himself that she wouldn't be here. A small town festival wouldn't exactly be the princess's style. But still, he kept looking for that slick fall of ash hair or the flash of some sort of clothing that no one else in Timber Bay would be wearing.

Of course, even if he did see her, what good would it do? She'd gotten rid of him the same night she'd gotten rid of her sling. Okay, yeah, that had been the plan all along. But, jeez—after that last night, he'd thought—he shook his head. What a yokel he was. To think her response to him had been special—just because his response to her had been special. For all he knew, she let herself go like that with every man that came along despite what she'd said. *Humpf.* Just as well if the princess didn't show up at the festival. He didn't need to feel like a damn fool all over again.

"They ran out of boxes," Molly said when she came back.

"Huh?" Lukas asked, scanning the crowd even more earnestly now that he'd decided to hightail it in the opposite direction if he saw her.

"Bakery boxes," Molly said, lifting a pumpkin pie up for him to see. "They ran out."

"Oh, well—"

"What's got into you?" Molly asked.

"Huh?"

She shook her head. "Earth to Lukas—come in for a landing."

Lukas frowned. "If you're gonna start teasing me you can carry your own kid."

Chloe giggled and clapped. "Don't encourage him, pumpkin," Molly said.

"Don't you have to head back to the Sweet Buns booth?" Lukas asked. The coast still looked clear, but with every second his dread of running into Gillian spread inside of him like wood rot.

"Not till I've had my yearly caramel apple."

"Sis, you've already been through three ears of corn, a hot dog and a hunk of apple pie."

"And your point is?" Molly got in line at the caramel apple stand.

"My point is you can do without the apple."

"Hey, you're the one who's always saying that tradition is not to be toyed with. And speaking of toys, your head is swiveling and bobbing like one of those dogs people put in the back window of their cars. You looking for someone in particular?"

Lukas stopped swiveling and bobbing. "Who would I be looking for?"

"That was my question."

"Huh?" Lukas couldn't seem to keep his mind on the conversation at hand. And he sure wasn't going to be able to deal with his sister's curiosity if it had time to get really roused. She was like a terrier with its teeth in a pant leg once she decided she needed to know something. "I'm gonna take Chloe over to watch the games while you wait for your turn here," he said, then walked off before Molly could say anything. Chances were pretty slim that she'd leave the line and come after him. Not with the way Molly waited for those caramel apples every year.

As they stood and watched kids bob for apples, Chloe's dark eyes were so bright with curiosity and her giggle so contagious that Lukas found himself starting to relax his vigil. The princess wouldn't be caught dead in a scene like this, he thought as they moved on to the ring toss.

After about ten minutes, they started back for the apple stand. As they got closer, he could see that Molly was talking to someone. Looked like a kid. Probably one of the students from the high school that sometimes helped her at Sweet Buns.

"There's your mommy," he said as he tickled Chloe's belly. She laughed and he tickled her again.

"Here's my pumpkin," Molly said as they drew nearer. Then, "Look who I ran into, Lukas."

The kid turned.

It was Gillian. And his heart banged against his chest so hard he was surprised little Chloe wasn't jostled from the force of it.

She had that fall of hair tucked under a cap—that's why he hadn't known it was her. And she was dressed—well, he supposed she was dressed pretty much like everyone else at the festival. Denim. Flannel. But her face. No one else had that face.

And no one else had this effect on him, either. He felt jittery and tongue-tied and suddenly sweaty despite the wind off the bay.

"Hi, Chloe!" she said brightly to his niece while she

totally ignored him. He stood there like some kind of stump while she babbled at Chloe about how cute her costume was. Chloe seemed way too happy about it, as far as Lukas was concerned. He decided to ignore the situation and cast his gaze about, hoping for rescue. He saw Danny's Uncle Tuffy in the crowd and burst out laughing.

"What's so funny?" Molly asked.

"Uncle Tuffy over there," he said, jerking his chin in the right direction. "His costume is pretty wild—even for him!"

"That's not a costume," Gillian said in a voice that could have frozen the pumpkin pie Molly was holding.

"'Course it is," he insisted. "It's too funny-looking to be anything else."

"Well, it *is* something else," the princess said, crossing her arms and cocking her hip like a sassy teenager. "It happens to be a rain cape and hat that I designed. I call it Lavender Showers."

Lukas snorted. "It looks like something a girl should be wearing."

"That's because it *is* something a girl should be wearing."

Lukas felt anger swelling inside of him. "You sold Uncle Tuffy women's clothing? How could you take advantage of him like that just to make a buck? Tuffy might be a little—um—odd, but the whole town loves him, and if you think you can just—just—"

Gillian gasped. "How dare you suggest that I would take advantage of that sweet little man. Listen up, McCoy—" she poked a finger in his chest "—I didn't sell Uncle Tuffy anything!"

"But you just said—"

"I most certainly did not! And if you would stop yelling like a demented lumberjack and just listen for once, then maybe—"

"Demented lumberjack?" he interrupted. "Well, if you

weren't so busy being the princess from the big city, maybe you'd be saying something worth listening to!"

"Come on, you two," Molly said, while Chloe looked from one to the other with wide eyes and an open mouth. "You're fighting like a couple of children."

Chloe squealed in agreement.

Lukas took a quick look around. They were starting to attract attention. He moved up close to Gillian and lowered his voice. "All right, princess, if you didn't sell it to him, how come he's wearing it?"

"He won it in a drawing."

"A drawing?"

"That's right—a drawing. I decided to run a contest to try to get people to come into the shop. Uncle Tuffy's was the only entry."

"And you just decided not to tell him that it was made for a woman, is that it?"

"Well, I was going to—but he seemed so happy to have won and he wanted to wear it and—"

"And it wouldn't be bad publicity for Glad Rags, either, huh? You let an old man make a fool of himself just to fulfill your own ambition—"

Gillian gasped again. "Of all the sanctimonious, infuriating—"

"Don't forget demented," Lukas yelled.

"You—you—" Gillian started, but Lukas didn't get a chance to hear what else she thought of him, because Chloe suddenly leaned over, grabbed a fistful of filling from the pie in Molly's hand, and flung it. It hit Gillian right in the face.

"Chloe!" Molly yelled but Chloe was too busy squealing in delight to pay attention.

Lukas started to laugh. "Well, I guess we know whose side Chloe is—" Before he could finish, Chloe flung another fistful of filling, hitting Lukas right in the nose.

She squealed and clapped and screamed, "More—more!"

"No more, Chloe," Molly admonished. "That was not a nice thing to do." She shot Lukas a look angry enough to spill over onto Gillian. "But if I wasn't a mother right now, I'd say you both deserved it. I don't know why you two can't get along," she said, then stalked off with Chloe.

Lukas felt like a dope. He'd lost it again in front of Gillian. Why did he always have to act so out of character around her?

"You McCoys should be outlawed!" Gillian blurted out as she wiped her face with her hand.

She'd gotten most of the pumpkin off, but she still had a splotch of it on the end of her nose. "You've got a little right here—" Lukas started to reach out but she jumped back.

"Hands off, McCoy. I can't afford another sprain or stain! So just stay away!"

She stalked off into the night, leaving Lukas standing there with pie on his face.

8

OCTOBER HAD TURNED into November. Old, worn-out leaves rattled down Sheridan Road in a stiff wind that blew off the bay. Lukas turned the collar of his denim jacket up against it when he came out of the Sheridan Hotel, then glanced at Glad Rags across the street. Something new had been added. Gillian had plastered a sign across the window advertising a pre-Thanksgiving sale. It was such a brave, in-your-face sign—all decorated with leaves cut out of something silver and the words made of glitter—but it made Lukas sad to see it there. He had the awful feeling that a sign advertising a going-out-of-business sale would be next.

For a moment, he thought about crossing the street to see how she was doing. But he figured she'd probably toss him out on his ear so he kept to his side of the street all the way to Ludington Avenue, then crossed and went into Ludington Drugs.

He said hello to a couple of people on his way to the lunch counter then slid onto a stool and gave Clara his order.

"Finally off your tuna kick, I see," Clara said then went to put his order in. That was another thing that had him down. Still no sign of Tiger, the ungrateful eater of high-priced tuna sandwiches.

Well, he thought, at least work was going good. So far, nothing had come of Gavin Sheridan's threats to sell the hotel and Agnes Sheridan had learned to trust him and

Danny enough to give them free rein. In fact, she hadn't even been around to inspect their work for over a week. Timber Bay Building and Restoration had had to hire subcontractors for electrical and plumbing work and it felt good to give contracts to guys he'd known most of his life. There was plenty of money coming in, too. Enough to do some more work on his house plus help Danny out with his personal baby—restoring the Opera House.

Yup, business couldn't be better—but his social life sure sucked. He couldn't even hold on to a half-tailed cat—how had he expected to stand a chance with Gillian?

"How's tricks, Lukas?" Gertie Hartlet asked as she took the stool next to his. Without waiting for a reply she chuckled hoarsely and added, "Looks like our litigious little lady will be leaving town soon."

Lukas jerked his head around to face Gertie. "What makes you say that?" he managed to get out around the sudden lump that had risen in his throat.

"I've practically got a bird's eye view of her place from my office. And, believe me, that little lady spends a lot of her time alone. Mark my words, that Thanksgiving sale sign is going to turn into a going-out-of-business sign any day now."

Lukas felt himself bristle at the proclamation, even though he'd thought the same thing when he'd seen the sign. "You don't have to sound so happy about it."

There was the hiss of flame on tobacco as Gertie lit a cigarette, almost immediately followed by Clara grumbling, "Put that out or get out," as she slid Lukas's grilled ham and cheese in front of him.

"That woman is heartless," Gertie muttered before she took a drag for the road, then put the cigarette out on the floor. "And what's gotten into you?" she said to Lukas as she shoved him in the shoulder. "You should be just as happy to see that little lady go. Didn't she blab that she'd love to see the Sheridans sell the hotel to a chain? If that would have happened, that chain would have brought in their own contractors and you'd be out of a job. They'd probably even bring in their own people to run it. This town wouldn't benefit one damn bit—oh, except for Clemintine's niece who'd be peddling those overpriced clothes to all those city people. Always looking out for number one, that one."

Lukas was glad he hadn't gotten anything that required a fork because he might have used it on Gertie Hartlet. "Look, I didn't want Agnes Sheridan to sell the hotel, either, but Gillian was only thinking about what was right for her business. Same as you and me would. You can't blame her for that, now can you?"

Gertie looked dumbfounded, and rightfully so, Lukas supposed. That was a hell of an outburst for him. To keep from saying more, he picked his sandwich up and took a bite.

Clara's grilled ham and cheese was one of his favorites but today he could hardly swallow it. The battle going on inside of him didn't make for a good lunch companion. Usually, he decided where he stood on an issue and he stayed there. But lately it felt like he was as scattered as the fallen leaves on the street. He was relieved that it looked like the Sheridan Hotel wasn't going to become part of a chain and that he and Danny were going to be able to see the restoration through to the end. But he also felt sorry for Gillian.

Sure, he'd predicted all over town that Glad Rags would be out of business by the first snowfall. And when he'd said those words, he'd thought that's what he wanted— Gillian gone for good. But it was different now. Now he hated the idea of Glad Rags failing—and he hated the idea of Gillian disappearing from his life. But what could he do?

"Hey, Ina. What'll you have?" Clara asked as Ina Belway took the stool on the other side of him.

"A bowl of your chicken dumpling soup, Clara. I just came from a meeting of the Women of the Holy Flock and I'm badly in need of comfort food."

Gertie leaned forward to look around Lukas. "Trouble in paradise?" she asked.

"It's that Thanksgiving play, Gertie. As usual, everyone is bickering about which part they want."

His mother was one of the Women of the Holy flock so Lukas knew exactly what Ina was talking about. Every year, the women put on a play in the church basement to raise money for Christmas baskets for the needy. It had become Timber Bay's official opening of the Christmas season. For years they'd done the story of the first Thanksgiving, but the last few times they'd tried out some Shakespeare. Ticket sales had been dismal so this year they were going back to the Pilgrim/Native thing. Unfortunately, the costumes had disappeared and they had to start from scratch.

"And to top it off," Ina went on, "they want to stick me with the part of the turkey. Do you have any idea how long it'll take to make that costume? When am I supposed to find time for that? This is a busy time of year in the tavern business."

Gertie grunted. "That's 'cause most of us can't face all that family stuff completely sober."

"Yeah, well, I'd rather be behind the bar listening to the likes of you complain than behind a sewing machine any day of the week."

Lukas knew what a project the women made of that play every year. He had memories of coming home from school some years to find a half-dozen church ladies sewing in the dining room. His dad generally would make himself scarce and he and Molly would live on macaroni and cheese out of a box for the duration. Every time the Ladies of the Flock needed new costumes, someone would argue that they should hire a professional to make them. Then someone else would argue that it'd be wasteful to spend money that could go to the needy on something they could do themselves. The possibility of asking for donations would be raised, but—

An idea hit Lukas with such force that he straightened from his slump as though someone had shoved a wooden dowel up his spine. He threw money on the counter next to his uneaten sandwich, then ran all the way back to the hotel, jumped into his truck, and headed for his parents' house.

Even at the age of thirty, sometimes a fella still needed his mother.

GILLIAN WAS STARTING to run out of panty hose—the good ones she'd brought with her from out east. Given the fact that nobody ever came into the shop, she was also starting to resent having to put them on every day. On the other hand, she didn't want them to be gone, either. Chiefly because she could no longer afford hose of that quality. A girl trading downwards in the hierarchy of panty hose was a sign that further slides down the slope of life were ahead.

She wiggled into her next-to-last pair while Pirate dispassionately watched her from the middle of the bed.

"Believe me," she told the cat as she slipped a red boatneck tunic over her head, "I'm aware that this is probably wishful dressing, but a girl's got to try. Who knows? Maybe we'll get a customer today."

Pirate closed his eyes and lifted a paw to lick.

"You could try to be supportive," Gillian muttered as she stepped into the matching skirt. "You've got a stake in this, too, you know. If I run out of money, you run out of cat food."

Pirate went right on licking, obviously secure that someone would provide. Gillian wished she could be as optimistic.

She slipped on red pumps, then went into the kitchen

to make coffee. Taking a cup with her, she went downstairs and opened the shop, then spent the morning slashing her prices—for the third time.

She had a candy bar, the kind laced with peanuts and caramel, for lunch. Nature's most perfect food—cheap and loaded with calcium and protein. Even cheaper when bought in quantity so she planned to substitute one meal a day with them. Her mother was going to be happy to hear that Gillian was finally getting enough fiber in her diet, thanks to the fact that good old-fashioned oatmeal was also cheaper in quantity. For dinner she usually did something with tuna or eggs and took one of the vitamin pills that her mother had so prophetically sent her—along with a book called *One Hundred Ways With Hamburger*. All very boring.

She sighed and thought fondly of Lukas McCoy's sack of day-old cinnamon buns. But after a moment, she was just thinking of Lukas McCoy's buns. And his thighs. And his arms. And his mouth. She felt heat rushing through her as she thought of the way she'd gone crazy in his arms. She could only imagine what other delights he was capable of. She gave a wistful sigh. Maybe she would have found out firsthand if her arm hadn't healed so darn well.

Gillian leaned her elbows on the counter next to the cash register and rested her chin on her interlaced hands. She missed Lukas, even though the big lug was forever making her mad about something. Like when he'd accused her of having an ulterior motive in neglecting to tell Uncle Tuffy that the rain cape he'd won was made for a woman. He'd been totally unreasonable. She looked at the slipper chair and sighed again. When a man could make a woman feel the way he had made her feel right in that very chair, maybe it was in the woman's best interest to try to overlook a few shortcomings.

She'd never known a man with such clever hands. Such skill. The preview she'd had of Lukas McCoy, lover, just made her want to own the whole movie. The bell over the front door jangled and Gillian, her mind on the talents of Lukas McCoy, languidly turned her head.

When she saw who it was, she shot up straight as William Tell's arrow and blushed redder than the apple on his hapless victim's head. "Mrs. McCoy," she said, certain that the guilt was evident in her voice. "Um—welcome to Glad Rags."

"Call me Frannie," said Lukas's mother.

"Um—Frannie. And," she added as she turned to the other woman, "welcome to you, too, Mrs. Walker."

"Kate, dear."

"Kate. So nice to see you both again. What can I do for you?"

"Oh, we're just sort of browsing," Frannie said.

"Santa needs ideas, you know," Kate added in a stage whisper.

"Terrific. Let me know if I can help you in any way."

Gillian slipped into the back room and fanned her face with her hand. Nothing like daydreaming about having sex with a man, then having his mother walk in, to make a girl break out in a sweat. She drank from a bottle of water she kept on the worktable, took a couple of deep breaths, then went back out into the shop.

Frannie and Kate were over in the lingerie alcove with their heads together, whispering. Gillian hoped they weren't on some sort of scouting mission for the Church of the Holy Flock, out to rid the town of lurid underwear.

Suddenly Kate giggled and Frannie turned around and asked, "Is this what I think it is?"

She was holding up the black lace thong panties that had ended up in Lukas's mouth on the night they'd first kissed. Seeing them in his mother's hands Gillian felt wicked in a scarlet letter/town vixen sort of way. "Oh, those are thong underwear," she said, snatching them as nonchalantly as possible from Frannie's hands. She tossed the panties into a basket. "I'd love to show you ladies some hand-painted silk scarves I have in stock. An artist I know in Boston does them."

She headed for the counter where the scarves were on display, sure that Kate and Frannie were the kind of women that would politely follow along. She was right.

"Are they uncomfortable?" Kate asked sweetly.

"The scarves?" Gillian asked with a puzzled frown.

"No—the thong panties."

"Oh—" So they were back to the thongs. "Yes. Very. I personally never wear them."

Gillian went behind the counter and Frannie said quietly, "Kate, they're the ones that go up in your—um—"

Kate's hand flew to her mouth. "Oh, goodness. Yes. That *would* be uncomfortable."

Gillian decided not to contribute further to that particular conversation. Instead, she laid out several scarves and the ladies oohed and ahhed over them appropriately. They blanched slightly when they read the little silver price tags hanging off each one.

"Maybe we'll just look around some more," Frannie said apologetically.

Gillian wished she could slash the prices on the scarves. They suddenly seemed horribly overpriced. But she couldn't without the artist's consent.

"What on earth is this?" Kate asked, holding up a scrap of wool tweed.

"It's a wool tweed halter that can double as a micro miniskirt," Gillian told her. "It's part of my *Tweeds Can Be Fun* collection."

Kate looked unsure, then held it up to her waist. "Well, it would make a nice apron." Then she looked up hopefully and asked, "Do you have any aprons in stock, dear?"

Aprons. Gillian's heart sank. "No. Sorry. No aprons."

Kate looked sad. "Will you be getting any in for Christmas?"

Gillian was spared having to come up with an answer to that because Frannie said, "Will you look at these seams, Kate? Have you ever seen work any better than this?"

Kate bent her head to look at the silk shirt in Frannie's hands. "No, I don't believe I have ever seen work that good."

Gillian felt foolishly pleased. "Well, thank you," she said, modestly.

"We could use someone like you on the play committee down at church. We're having a dickens of a time with the costumes this year." Frannie looked up from a seam. "Do you ever do that kind of work, dear?"

"Costumes? Well—" Had it come to this? Was she going to have to take in *sewing*? Gillian quickly subtracted what she figured the heating bills were going to be for the winter if the wind kept blowing off the bay like it was today, from the balance in her bank account. Definitely in the red. Gillian hoped her pride wouldn't stick in her throat on the way down. "Of course," she said with a bright smile, wondering if the job would pay enough to get red meat back in her diet. "Back in New York I made costumes all the time. What did you have in mind?"

THE DAYS WERE GROWING shorter. It was just after five o'clock but the desk lamp was already lit at Timber Bay Building and Restoration. Lukas and Danny were sitting in the office, sucking down a couple of beers and discussing the next phase of renovations at the Sheridan Hotel.

"We should be far enough along to take a break over Christmas, don't you think?" Danny asked. "Hannah wants us to go down to southern Illinois to visit her father."

Lukas shrugged. "Don't see why not. Mrs. Sheridan hasn't been around lately so it's not like she's breathing down our necks or anything."

"She has been kind of absent, hasn't she?"

"Yeah. I was hoping she wasn't going to show up this afternoon when you were missing. Where'd you go after lunch, anyway?"

Danny got a big grin on his face. "Did a little early Christmas shopping. I went over to the jewelry store and put some diamond earrings for Hannah on layaway."

Lukas whistled. "Nice."

"The way things are going, I should be able to pay for them long before Christmas."

"You might want to save your money, Walker," came a voice from the doorway.

Lukas could smell Gavin Sheridan's cologne as soon as he stepped inside.

"Well, look what slithered in, silent as a snake," Danny said. "And what business is it of yours if I save my money or not?"

Gavin shrugged. "Just a friendly warning. After you read this," he held out a long, cream-colored envelope, "you'll understand why."

Lukas looked at the envelope, then at Danny.

"What's the matter?" Gavin asked. "Can't either of you read?"

Danny swore as he stood up, grabbed the envelope out of Gavin's hand, and tore it open. He read silently for several seconds, then looked up. "You expect us to believe this piece of paper? It's bogus, Sheridan. No way did your granny sign that thing."

But Lukas could see that Danny was thrown. The tension coming off his body was almost visible. "What's in the letter, Danny?" he asked.

It was Gavin who answered. "It's a letter from my grandmother, McCoy, ordering you to stop work on the hotel immediately."

Lukas shot to his feet. "What? What reason would she have to do that? She's satisfied with our work."

"But I'm not," Sheridan said.

"Our contract is with her," Danny pointed out.

"Yes, it is," Gavin said mildly. "That's why the letter is from her. Now, hand over your keys."

"Like hell we will," Lukas said. "Not without talking to your grandmother first."

"If she wanted to talk to you, she wouldn't have sent me as her errand boy, would she? Now why don't you be good boys and hand over your keys so you can get back to whittling and swilling beer."

Danny lunged for Gavin and Lukas lunged for Danny.

"Danny, come on—that won't do any good."

"But it'll feel damn good, buddy," Danny said as he struggled against Lukas's hold.

"Let him go, big guy," Sheridan said. "He lays one finger on me, I go right to the police station and have him arrested."

"Like you'd be able to walk if I let him go," scoffed Lukas. "Now get the hell out of here before I decide to grant your request."

Lukas held on to Danny until he heard Sheridan's car start up out in the driveway, then he pushed him into a chair.

"Stay right there and cool down."

"You should have let me at him," Danny said.

"Yeah. Hannah would love to have to go down to the jail and bail you out."

Danny gave a short bark of laughter. "I see your point, buddy. So do you have a better idea?"

"For starters, I suggest we pay a visit to Agnes and find out what's going on."

"Yeah, let's hear it right from the dragon's mouth."

Fifteen minutes later they were climbing the wrought-iron fence that surrounded the Sheridan estate.

"Damn," Danny groaned. "I hope this is the last time I'm going to have to do this."

"Why do you think the chauffeur wouldn't let us in?" Lukas asked as he jumped down on the other side.

"Orders from Timber Bay's favorite son would be my guess," Danny said after he'd joined Lukas.

"Come on. Let's move. I want to get to her before Gavin gets back."

The chauffeur opened the door and Lukas could have sworn that he was glad to see them.

"Look," Danny started, "we know you've got orders not to let us in, but—"

"On the contrary," Hampton stated. "My orders merely say not to let you on the grounds. I'm afraid Mr. Gavin did not leave any instructions in the event that you found your own way in." He opened the door wider and stood back. "Madam is in the sitting room to your right. Good luck. I hope you can change her mind about selling the hotel."

Lukas did a double take. "What did you say?"

"I'm sorry, sir, I thought you knew," Hampton said. "Mr. Gavin has persuaded Madam to sell."

"Of all the two-timing, underhanded—"

"Easy, Danny," Lukas said. "Maybe you should let me handle this."

Danny looked like he was going to give him a fight, then he shrugged. "Okay—you're the one who knows how to sweet-talk her. I'll just keep my mouth shut."

"That'll be the day," Lukas muttered.

"I'll be nearby if you should need me," Hampton said before quietly disappearing around a corner.

"That guy gives me the creeps," Danny said.

"Behave yourself." Lukas opened the sitting-room door.

Danny walked in ahead of him and immediately started to misbehave.

"Your telephone out of order, Mrs. Sheridan?" Danny

asked. "Or did you just think it was none of our business if you sold the hotel?"

"Damn, Danny, I thought you were going to let me handle this," Lukas muttered.

Agnes Sheridan rose from her chair. "Hampton!" she shouted, before turning her steel eyes on them. "How did you get in here? I thought Gavin was going to deal with you."

"Don't blame Jeeves," Danny said, "we climbed the fence."

"Remind me to have barbed wire installed," Agnes said dryly. "Now would you please leave."

Danny started to say something, but Lukas stuck out his arm and clamped his palm over his partner's mouth.

"If you don't mind, Mrs. Sheridan, I think you owe us an explanation."

"I owe you nothing," she said imperiously.

"Sure you do. Says so in the contract."

"Didn't my grandson tell you? After the sale of the hotel, that contract will be worthless."

"Then it's true?" Danny yelled, pushing Lukas's hand away.

Lukas gave him a look, pointed at a chair and said, "Sit."

Danny wisely sat.

Lukas turned back to Mrs. Sheridan. "Why would you sell the hotel? You love that place. And you've waited a long time to revive it."

The fight seemed to go out of her as she let go of the steel in her back and sank back into her chair. "I'm moving away," she said dully. "Chicago. Gavin bought me a condo that—"

"You're talking nonsense," Lukas said. "You don't belong in Chicago any more than I do. You belong right here in Timber Bay."

Agnes shook her head. "Gavin is the one who belongs here. That was the dream, you know. Renovate the hotel, make it beautiful again to lure Gavin back to run it. But, I can see now that that will never happen."

Lukas worked his jaw for a moment, trying to rein in the anger that was starting to flood him. "So you're just going to give up?"

"I'm tired of fighting, Lukas. I've been fighting all my life and I want some peace before I die. And if that means giving up on this town and moving to Chicago, then that's what I'm going to do. I've tried to keep the Sheridan family name alive in Timber Bay almost single-handedly. And for what? The Sheridan men leave and never look back. If they don't care—why should I?"

"Nice try," Danny said, "but pure bull."

Lukas shot Danny a look over his shoulder. "I thought you were going to let me handle this?"

"Not if you're going to fall for that load. Agnes here is more a Sheridan than if she'd been born with their blood. She'd never give up her place in this town without a fight." Danny stood up and came to stand beside Lukas. "Gavin threatened you, didn't he?"

Agnes drew herself up. "Don't be absurd," she insisted imperiously.

"Come on," Danny cajoled. "Why else would you be doing this? Gavin has threatened to have you declared incompetent if you don't do what he says—he said as much when he came to town last month. Remember, Lukas?"

Yes, Lukas remembered. "Is that true?" he asked Agnes.

She hesitated, running her fingers back and forth over the tooled silver handle of her cane. Finally she said, "Very well—if you must know, yes. It's true."

Lukas knew it cost her to admit it. "Excuse me for saying so, Mrs. Sheridan, but that's a load of crap. You're no more incompetent than I am."

Agnes gave a big sigh. "My grandson has very powerful lawyers—and I've made mistakes over the years."

"So who hasn't?" Danny said. "There's not a judge in the world who would say that you don't know what you're doing. Gavin would never win this one."

"Gavin strongly thinks he'll prevail."

"He's bluffing," Lukas insisted. "Call him on it. What could he possibly have on you that's so bad?"

Agnes paused and for a moment Lukas thought she wasn't going to answer. "The legend," she finally said.

Lukas screwed his face up in puzzlement. "The legend of the Tunnel of Love?"

Agnes nodded. "He says that the fact that I had one end of the tunnel sealed off after his grandfather ran off with that waitress proves that I believe in the legend. He says that that would be enough to convince a judge that my reasoning is in question."

"Yeah, maybe after he paid the judge enough," Danny muttered.

"Good point, Mr. Walker. Now you see what I'm up against. But even more than that, I can't bear the thought of having all that dredged up in open court again. I prefer the skeletons stayed in the closet." She stood. "I appreciate your coming, but the wheels are already in motion and I am far too weary to try to stop them."

Lukas didn't know what to say. He stood there with his mouth hanging open while Agnes Sheridan walked slowly out of the room.

"Man, I never thought I'd say it," Danny said, "but I like it better when the Dragon Lady is yelling at us."

"I hear ya," Lukas said. In fact, he thought it was damn eerie seeing Agnes Sheridan give up. "What should we do?"

Danny shrugged. "I guess we better find a lawyer tomorrow. But right now, let's go find Jeeves. I hope he has no orders about letting us out of the grounds because I sure don't want to have to climb that fence again."

9

GILLIAN WAS LEANING on the counter at Glad Rags, languidly paging through the latest copy of *Vogue*, when the bell over the shop door jangled and in walked two women, one blond and one brunette, who could not possibly be natives. By their chic haircuts and gorgeously cut clothes, Gillian quickly identified the species. *Customers*. Real customers. She was suddenly very glad she'd chosen to wear her Chanel-inspired pink tweed suit with the faux white-fox collar from her *Tweeds Can Be Fun* collection and her rose-colored stilettos, despite the fact that her feet were mad as hell at her for putting them through the torture.

"Hello, ladies. Welcome to Glad Rags," she said as she came out from behind the counter, trying not to wince with every step. "I'm Gillian Caine. Please let me know if I can help you in any way."

"We'll just browse, thank you," the blond one said without even looking at her.

"Oh, we love browsers," Gillian enthused, but it was obvious neither woman intended to pay any attention to her. Fine. It wasn't a popularity contest. Just as long as they bought something. And really—her clothes could sell themselves when the right person came along.

Gillian retreated back behind the counter and started flipping through *Vogue* again until a squeal nearly made her topple off her stilettos.

"Maxie! Look at this absolutely adorable little skirt."

Gillian grinned. Just as she thought, the visiting species were natural hunters. She craned her neck to see what had prompted the squeal and grinned. The brunette was practically melting all over the *Urban Flannel* collection.

"Never mind that—take a look at this silver sheath," said Maxie as she held up the very dress Gillian had worn the day she'd let Lukas out of prison. How Gillian would love to sell it and never have to look at it again.

She came out from behind the counter. "Why don't I hang that in the dressing room for you," she said, taking the dress from the blonde. "And have you seen the rest of that collection? There's a darling duster that looks terrific over the dress—"

An hour later, clothes were strewn all over the shop and Gillian was actually behind the cash register for a change. Sales! Finally! She hadn't been this excited since—since—oh, never mind. She was not going to let Lukas spoil this moment of success for her.

"Who would have thought it, Quinn," said the blonde to the brunette, "that we'd find anything even remotely cutting-edge so far north of Chicago?"

Gillian, searching for a price tag on a camisole, winced at the *remotely*, but decided it was a compliment, anyway. After all, they were actually *buying*.

"Seriously," Quinn said, "this place and that coffee shop across the street are the only real signs of civilization."

"Well, that is," Maxie reminded her, "until Brunswick opens its newest."

Gillian's fingers stopped punching keys on the cash register. "Brunswick Hotels?" she asked. "Are they opening a hotel in this area?"

Quinn sniffed and gave Gillian a *not that it's any of your business* look. "The company hopes to issue a press release soon," she said stiffly.

Maxie laughed. "In other words, we're not yet authorized to say. But we're in PR at Brunswick," she said with a wink. "I think you can put the rest together."

Gillian beamed. *Yes!* She could put it together, all right. Agnes Sheridan was selling the hotel to the Brunswick chain. And that meant that she'd be seeing more of *species: customer*, in the future.

As she wrapped the silver dress in tissue, she said, "I design most of the inventory myself, you know."

Quinn studied her more shrewdly. "Really?"

"I'm the Gillian on the label," she pointed out. *"Glad Rags by Gillian."*

"How interesting. I think you'll be pleased when you hear the press release. It should be very good for your business."

"When do you think the hotel will open?" Gillian asked.

"I don't believe I have said a hotel will be opening," Quinn said with a superior little smile.

Maxie didn't seem at all to share her colleague's reticence. "Between you and us," she said in a phony whisper, "the property Brunswick is in the process of acquiring is a mess. Some locals have been working on it and we're going to have to undo a lot of what they've done."

Gillian frowned. *Undo?* "Like what?" she asked.

"Well, if you've ever stayed in a Brunswick hotel, you'd know that all the hotels have the signature Brunswick staircase in the lobby."

Quinn was studying Gillian dubiously. *"Have* you ever stayed at a Brunswick?" she asked.

"Yes, of course. The staircases are marble—cold, white marble."

"Yes," Quinn agreed. "Very sophisticated. So the oak banister will have to go—"

Gillian blinked. "Excuse me, but that banister is a work of art. I know the man who did the restorations and they're completely authentic. The whole lobby is gorgeous."

"That may be, but it's not a Brunswick if it doesn't have the staircase," Quinn said.

"And don't forget that huge, drafty ballroom," Maxie added.

"What about the ballroom?" Gillian asked.

"It's going to be divided up to enlarge the lobby and the restaurant."

"What?" Gillian screeched. "Divided? But that room is beautiful—and so full of history."

The two women exchanged a look. "Gavin said the locals found it hard to accept change," Maxie said under her breath.

Locals? They thought she was a local? Gillian opened her mouth to correct the assumption, but then started thinking about Lukas's beautiful banister being ripped out and it was all she could do to finish ringing up the sale.

By the time the women left, her spirits were sagging more than a cheap pair of panty hose.

"This is ridiculous," she muttered to herself. She'd just made a very huge sale. When she added it to the money she was earning for making costumes for the Women of the Holy Flock, she'd have enough to keep her going for a while. And wasn't this just the beginning? There would be other visitors from *planet chic* if a new Brunswick Hotel opened. And that could only bring success. And that would prove, without a doubt, that she didn't need a man to make it in this world.

Okay, this was better. Now she was excited.

And then she thought about that banister again.

All the hours Lukas had put in on it. It was a shame. But she had to look after **her**self, didn't she? Isn't that what she'd learned from Ryan? *Only the strong survive.* Well, in Ryan's case, only the most devious—but the point was the same. Everyone had to look out for himself. She couldn't afford to be sentimental about a vine-covered banister—or about the man who had carved it.

PHILO HERNSHAW HUMMED while he read. That, coupled with the fact that he had to be the slowest reader Lukas had ever seen, was making Lukas wish he'd had decaffeinated for breakfast. It didn't help that every thirty seconds he stopped to fiddle with his brand-new hearing aid.

"Mmm," Philo hummed, and Danny and Lukas looked at each other. "Umm," he hummed again. "Mmmhmm."

Finally, he put the pages down, took off his glasses, and started using his superwide necktie with the stags leaping across it to clean them.

Once again, Lukas wished they could have gotten an appointment with another lawyer. And not just because Philo was a slow reader. The fact that Philo had been Gillian's lawyer—even though he'd never actually made it to court—was making Lukas remember too many things he wanted to forget.

"Well?" Danny prodded impatiently.

Philo put his glasses back on, then sadly shook his head. "I'm afraid there really isn't much I can do for you," he said apologetically. "The contract states that if the deed to the property changes hands, all previous contracts are null and void."

Danny sighed heavily. "Guess I better take those diamond earrings off layaway."

"Now, hold on," Lukas told him, then turned to Philo. "You're sure there's nothing we can do?"

"You can, of course, sue for any unpaid expenses and materials, but short of that—"

"It's not just the money," Lukas started to explain.

"It's not?" Danny asked.

"Come on, Danny, you know it isn't. Mr. Hernshaw, if that sale goes through, Sheridan Hotel will never be restored to its past glory. And I swear to you, that's what Agnes Sheridan wanted. That's all she ever talked about."

Philo Hernshaw smiled sadly. "But, you see, Agnes is authorizing the sale and it's her signature on the letter directing you to stop working on the hotel. So unless you can come up with a valid reason—oh—let's say you could prove that the grandson is exerting some sort of undue influence over her— but I warn you that would be very costly. Very costly, indeed. And without Agnes's cooperation, I'm afraid it would be next to impossible, anyway. So short of changing Agnes's mind, I'm afraid there really isn't anything you can do."

Lukas leaned forward. "Mr. Hernshaw, you've known Agnes Sheridan a long time, haven't you?"

"My, yes. I had business dealings with her over the years. A very formidable woman."

"What do you think it would take to make her change her mind?" Lukas asked.

"Oh, my," the mild-mannered lawyer said. "I'm afraid it would take a miracle."

"TURN AROUND," Gillian said, "and let me check your feathers."

Ina Belway stood on the stool in the middle of Aunt Clemintine's living room; big, multicolored feathers made of felt fanning out around her backside, while the rest of the Women of the Church of the Holy Flock were scattered about, drinking coffee and nibbling from the trays of goodies they always brought along to a fitting.

"Perfect," Gillian declared. "You're all done, Ina."

"About time. Now what did you do with Kate's brownies?"

"Kitchen, I think."

"I'm so sorry about that seam, dear," Kate said, as she came out of the bedroom and handed Gillian her Pilgrim costume.

"No problem. Better to have it burst here than on stage."

"She's right about that," Frannie McCoy said. "We don't want the Thanksgiving play to become X-rated." The ladies of The Flock, most of them quite obviously more prudish than Frannie, tittered and gasped.

Gillian was still getting used to the idea of Lukas's mother in her living room. In fact, it was still surprising to come into the room and see the Women of the Holy Flock, in various forms of undress, looking like a band of Pilgrim strippers.

Gillian hadn't wanted to take the job they'd offered. She'd cried herself to sleep the night she had agreed to do the costumes. But much to her surprise, she was enjoying her time with them. They were a lively group and she admired their dedication to the cause. She'd already bought tickets for the Thanksgiving Eve performance.

"I think I'm due for a brownie break, too," she told the ladies, then headed for the kitchen.

"She's turned out to be such a sweetheart, Hannah," Ina was saying as she leaned on the kitchen counter next to Hannah, "that I wish the accident did qualify them for the legend. But in my book, it just doesn't."

"What legend?" Gillian asked.

Ina and Hannah exchanged meaningful looks before Ina shrugged. "Oh, nothing," she said dismissively before taking a big bite of the brownie in her hand.

"Come on, you two. It's not *nothing*. Now, tell."

"Well, you see—" Hannah began.

"Hannah—" Ina warned.

"Why shouldn't she know?" Hannah asked. "The legend is real. Look at what happened to Danny and me. Gillian not knowing about it may be keeping them apart."

Gillian knew Kate put bourbon in her mincemeat, and now she wondered if she put anything in her brownies. This conversation wasn't making any sense. "Who could I possibly be keeping apart?"

Hannah seemed to be weighing the decision to tell her,

so Gillian smiled encouragingly. "Come on, Hannah," she said. "Who would I keep apart?"

"You and Lukas," Hannah finally said.

"Excuse me?" Gillian asked even as her heart jolted at the sound of his name. "There *is* no Lukas and me."

"And that's exactly why you should know about the legend!" Hannah exclaimed.

Gillian pulled out two of Aunt Clemintine's chrome kitchen chairs. "Sit," she commanded. When they had, she took a third chair. "Now, spill. What is this legend?"

"It's called the legend of the Tunnel of Love," Hannah answered.

Gillian wasn't sure she'd heard right. "Tunnel of love?"

"There's this tunnel that runs under the street, between the hotel and the opera house." Ina picked crumbs off the plate of brownies in the middle of the table. "One of the Sheridan men had it built around the turn of the century so he could diddle his favorite opera singer whenever she came to town."

"Diddle? How romantic," Gillian drawled as she chose a brownie from the plate.

"Ha! I could put it even less romantically if the ladies of The Flock weren't flocking all over your living room," Ina said before plucking another brownie for herself.

Hannah gave her a look, then took up the story. "The legend says that if the tunnel brings two people together, they are destined to be together for all time."

"Come on." Gillian licked frosting off her fingers. "Get serious."

"That's what I thought at first, too," Hannah said. "But the legend certainly worked for Danny and me. It was while we were trapped in the tunnel that he first kissed me. We thought we didn't even like each other at the time."

"Sorry—I don't get what this has to do with me and Lukas."

"Some of the townsfolk think that you and Lukas qualify for the legend," Ina said. "But I think that's bull, excuse the expression."

Gillian frowned. "I didn't even know about the tunnel so how could Lukas and I qualify?"

"The night of your accident, Lukas was coming out of the tunnel by way of that manhole cover," Hannah explained. "There are people in town who think that's the same as the tunnel bringing you together."

"That's nonsense," Gillian insisted.

"Damn straight," Ina agreed.

"And there are obviously those who don't agree," Hannah added dryly.

"Either way," Ina said, "there's been a lot of speculation around town about it."

Swell, thought Gillian. This was worse than the *love-slave* thing.

"You make it sound like the whole town is watching to see which side turns out to be right."

Ina shrugged. "Not a lot to do in Timber Bay between the Harvest Festival and the Christmas season."

Oh, terrific. She and Lukas were the half-time entertainment between one holiday and another. The only way this could get worse was if they made her sing The Star-Spangled Banner. Time for squelching.

"Look," she said empathetically, "even if we did qualify, all it would prove is that the legend is bogus. Lukas and I don't even get along. All we ever do is fight." Which wasn't exactly true, but things could only get worse if people knew how easily she swooned over the big lug. But it was only physical. He was, after all, a big, hot hunk of man. Love had nothing at all to do with it.

"Well, as I said," Hannah pointed out, "Danny and I didn't get along at first, either."

"Forget it, Hannah," Ina said, "she's not buying it."

"You're absolutely right, Ina," said Gillian. "And I'd

appreciate it if the two of you will tell everyone else in town that they better start watching for the next victims of the tunnel, because Lukas and I definitely do not qualify."

"Speaking of victims of the tunnel," Hannah said. "Danny told me why Agnes Sheridan agreed to sell the hotel."

"Really?" Ina asked eagerly.

Hannah nodded.

"Well, come on, spill," Ina demanded.

"Danny told me that Gavin threatened to have her declared incompetent if she didn't sell and move to Chicago."

"Incompetent?" Gillian snorted. "I only met her once but she seemed to be playing with more than a full deck."

"Oh, she is," Hannah agreed. "But that's where the tunnel comes in. Gavin claimed that all he'd have to do is tell a judge that Agnes believes in the Tunnel of Love and he'd be awarded power of attorney for not just the hotel but everything else she owns, as well."

"You're telling me that that crotchety old woman believes in this legend?" Gillian asked.

"Enough to have one end of it sealed when her husband ran off with a waitress from the hotel, same as his father before him did," Ina explained.

"Except he ran off with an opera singer," Hannah added.

"The only reason," Ina went on, "that the hotel end of the tunnel isn't sealed is because there's electrical and plumbing stuff in there that has to be accessible."

"So what you're saying," Gillian said, "is that the fact that she had the tunnel sealed is what her grandson intends to use to prove she's too batty to know what she's doing?"

"Exactly." Hannah bobbed her head.

"But that's so unfair," Gillian cried. "Isn't there anything anyone can do?"

Hannah shrugged. "I've been wracking my brain trying

to come up with something. I even thought about offering to testify in court about Danny and me, if it comes to that."

"You mean about the legend coming true for you?" Gillian asked.

Hannah nodded.

"Do you think that would help?"

Hannah shrugged again. "Who knows? But it seems to me if they could declare a woman incompetent because she believes in a legend, why wouldn't they take testimony that the legend really does exist into consideration? Probably a long shot. But I'm fond of Agnes and I'd be willing to give it a go."

"Have you told Mrs. Sheridan about your theory and your willingness to help?"

"No," Hannah answered. "You think I should?"

"Absolutely. Maybe if she knows someone is on her side it'll make all the difference."

"I think Gillian's right, Hannah," Ina put in.

"You really think I should go talk to her?"

"Absolutely!" Gillian said.

"Oh—I don't know. Something tells me that Agnes Sheridan wouldn't be happy about anyone prying into her life."

"So what?" Gillian threw up her hands in exasperation. "There's a lot at stake here."

"You're right," Hannah said. "But still—"

"Tell you what—I'll even go with you."

Hannah grabbed Gillian's hand and gave it an enthusiastic squeeze. "Oh, Gillian, that would be great."

While Hannah and Ina plotted the when, where and how of the meeting with Agnes Sheridan, Gillian grabbed another brownie and wondered what the hell she was doing. Whose side was she on, anyway? If Brunswick didn't buy the Sheridan Hotel, there'd be no more sophisticated shoppers from Chicago, which might mean no more Glad Rags. But how on earth would she be able to enjoy any success she might have if she'd gained it at the expense of an old woman's dignity?

GILLIAN TOSSED and turned half the night, wondering if she was doing the right thing. But the next morning she met Hannah at Sweet Buns, as promised.

"Going into the Dragon's den, I hear," Molly said as she poured coffee.

"Afraid so," Hannah admitted. "Seemed like a good idea last night. This morning, I'm not so sure."

Gillian silently agreed. This morning, she wasn't sure about anything.

"Well, don't go in there unarmed," Molly said. "I'll box up some sweet buns for you to take along. If that doesn't subdue the beast, nothing will."

With the white bakery box tied with green string on the front seat between them and Hannah behind the wheel of Danny's pickup, Gillian and Hannah drove to the Sheridan estate.

"Madam is not receiving today," a deep voice crackled over the intercom that was mounted on the locked wrought-iron gate.

"We intend to talk to Mrs. Sheridan, Hampton. So you might as well let us in or I'll just climb the fence again."

The gates opened.

"I'd like to hear the rest of that story sometime," Gillian said dryly as they drove through.

Hannah laughed. "Danny and I had a very unusual courtship."

"I'm not surprised. I've met some of his family."

"Eccentric is their middle name." Hannah drove up the curved driveway and parked the car. "God, I hope this works," she said as she cut the engine.

Gillian took a deep breath. "Me, too."

Hannah looked at her curiously. "You know, Danny

told me that you and Lukas were on opposite sides of the fence on this one."

"We were," Gillian admitted. "We even fought about it. But what Gavin Sheridan is doing isn't right. So even though I might be signing Glad Rags's death warrant, I'd never forgive myself if I didn't do something to help." And, she told only herself, she didn't think she could bear it if Lukas's beautiful banister was replaced with cold white marble.

Hannah smiled at her. "I can see why Molly likes you so much."

Gillian didn't know what to say to that. She wasn't used to people in Timber Bay liking her. So she just said, "Come on, let's go."

They got out of the car, walked up to the door and rang the bell.

Hampton, apparently both the chauffeur and the butler, showed them into what he called the *morning room*, then went off to see if the lady of the house would *receive them*, as he put it.

"I wonder if she rescued him from the morgue," Gillian whispered.

"Shh," Hannah hissed. "You're as bad as Danny."

"Hey, you're the one who climbed the fence."

Hannah wrinkled her nose. "I know—isn't that weird? This town seems to have an odd effect on people."

"Tell me about it," muttered Gillian. "I'm about to cut off my nose to spite my face."

The door opened and Agnes Sheridan, her cane plunking against the floor, entered.

"Hannah, my dear, how nice of you to stop by. But I'm not really up to—" Agnes's eyes lit on Gillian. "Aren't you—?"

"The girl who sued Lukas McCoy," Gillian finished for her. "Right. That would be me. But I think I'm about to make amends, Mrs. Sheridan, if you'll hear us out."

"Hannah, are you friends with this creature?" the old lady asked sternly.

"Yes, I am, Mrs. Sheridan. And I hope you'll let both of us talk to you."

The old lady had been scrutinizing Gillian for several uncomfortable seconds when Gillian remembered the bakery box in her hand. "We brought you some of Molly's sweet buns," she said, holding out the box.

Agnes grunted. "Girl makes wonderful bran muffins—"

"Oh, you'll like these even better, Mrs. Sheridan," Gillian assured her.

"Put them there," Mrs. Sheridan commanded, pointing to a side table with her cane. Gillian did as ordered. Then she pointed at two matching wingback chairs and said, "Sit."

Gillian and Hannah sat.

Mrs. Sheridan took the stiff-backed chair opposite the wingbacks. "Now tell me why you're here, despite the fact that I don't wish for you to be."

Hannah cleared her throat. "We're here to offer our support and to beseech you to consider changing your mind about selling the hotel."

"I'm afraid that's impossible."

"And I'm afraid that's negative," Gillian countered. "With that attitude, no wonder your grandson is getting the better of you."

"Gillian!" Hannah gasped.

Gillian ignored her and went on. "Mrs. Sheridan, since you seem so fond of being blunt, I intend to do the same. You seemed feisty enough that day at the hospital when you told me off. Where has your fight gone? Why are you letting your grandson get away with this?"

Agnes Sheridan stared at her long and hard before saying, "A wise woman knows when she can't win."

"But a brave woman never stops trying," Gillian said.

And before she knew it she was blurting out her life story to this stern, dignified old woman who didn't even like her. She told her about Ryan and about losing the business she thought was half hers. She told her about her hopes and dreams and how she had lost them but then picked herself right back up again and started over.

"I vowed to never again let another man run my life. And you should do the same thing."

There, thought Gillian. She'd said it. She sat back and waited for a haranguing. But when the old lady finally spoke, she merely sounded weary.

"Young woman, you are absolutely right. I should. But I won't." She shook her head and there was a ghost of a smile at her lips. "Oh, when I was younger, I was very like you. No one got the better of me. But I'm afraid that in this case, I've got nothing left to fight with. If Gavin testifies in court that I—"

"Yes, yes," Gillian interrupted impatiently. "We know all about that. He says he can prove in court that you believe in the legend and therefore you're incompetent to handle your own affairs. But that's why we're here. Hannah is prepared to back you up. She's prepared to testify in court that the legend is real because it came true for her and Danny."

Gillian swore there were actual tears shining in the old lady's eyes when she turned to look at Hannah. "Hannah, my dear, I'll never forget this gesture. But don't you see? One voice would never be enough to—'"

"How about two voices?" Gillian asked.

Both women turned to look at her.

"Two voices?" Hannah asked.

Gillian swallowed hard. "Well—maybe more like one and a half. You see, the fact is, the tunnel brought Lukas and me together, too—" she bit her lip "—sort of."

Hannah looked confused. "But you and Lukas are always protesting that you don't even like each other."

"I know—and we don't—but—um—*strange* things happened whenever we were alone in that shop at night."

"Strange things?" Hannah asked, wrinkling her brow. "You mean like ghosts?"

Agnes Sheridan gave a dry cackle of laughter. "I think she's talking about sex."

Gillian grinned. "See? I knew there was nothing wrong with your mind."

The old woman's eyes twinkled.

"You and Lukas had sex in the dress shop?" Hannah whispered incredulously.

"Well, no—I mean, yes—well—let's just say that *stuff* happened." She smiled. "Pretty magical stuff, actually. Stuff that made no sense. Which is why I believe that there might be something to the legend."

"And you're willing to go before a judge and testify that these inexplicable—er—happenings between you and Lukas McCoy were caused by the legend?"

Gillian nodded. "I mean, the legend obviously didn't take all that well with Lukas and me, so alone it's not much. But add it to Hannah's story and maybe it will help."

Agnes studied her for a moment. "You're not so different from Clemintine after all, are you?"

Gillian thought she just might cry. "I hope not."

Agnes shook her head. "I'm afraid it still won't be enough. Gavin made other assertions—things he claims he can use against me in court. He's saying I've squandered a fortune on restoring the hotel—in part because I've hired unqualified locals who are robbing me blind."

Gillian jumped to her feet. "Lukas and Danny? That's a lie!"

"Of course it's a lie," Hannah said more calmly. "Mrs.

Sheridan, all a court would have to do is look at the company's books—"

"And anyone with eyes can see that they're qualified," Gillian argued. "Why, Lukas is an artist. Have you seen that banister he restored? Why, it's gorgeous—a work of art—and Brunswick is just going to rip it out. After Lukas spent weeks, lovingly paying attention to detail. I've seen him work, Mrs. Sheridan, and it's like he's making love to the wood. It's like—" Gillian became aware that both Hannah and Mrs. Sheridan were watching her with some bemusement. She shut her mouth and sat down.

"A very impassioned speech, Miss Caine. And I agree. Lukas is an artist. We can readily prove that, too."

"Well, then—" Gillian began.

"Gavin also plans to charge that I have become a recluse, uninterested in life—"

Gillian flapped her hand. "Well, that one's easy. We can start proving him wrong about that right away."

"We can?" Hannah asked a little anxiously.

"Sure. We can start by finding her a part in the Thanksgiving play at the Church of the Holy Flock. They can always use another pilgrim. I'll start making your costume today. The next group fitting is day after tomorrow. Be there—and don't forget to bring a goodie to pass around. Next?"

Agnes looked at Hannah. "She is very persistent, isn't she?"

"Yes," Hannah agreed. "She is."

"Lukas could do worse," Agnes Sheridan pronounced.

Minutes later Gillian and Hannah were driving back through the wrought-iron gate, with a promise from Agnes that she would at least consider fighting Gavin on the sale.

"I nearly burst out laughing when you said the Flock could always use another pilgrim. Somehow I can't see

Agnes Sheridan shucking corn on the makeshift stage in the basement of the church."

Gillian laughed. "It'll do her good."

"You know," Hannah said after a moment, "Mrs. Sheridan was right."

"About what?" Gillian asked.

"Lukas could do worse."

Gillian was surprised by the comment. "Thanks, Hannah, but I'm sure he doesn't see it that way."

"How do you know?"

"Well, because all we do is fight."

"But you said that at the shop at night *stuff* happened."

"Yeah, but don't you think never leaving the shop would be a slightly confining way to live?"

Hannah laughed. "I suppose so. Maybe you should go out on a date with him and see what happens."

"Huh—like he would ask me out in this lifetime," Gillian muttered.

Hannah shrugged. "So why don't *you* ask *him?*"

The idea appalled Gillian. "I could never—not in a million years!"

"Come on—the way you handled Agnes Sheridan just now? You were pretty aggressive. It's hard for me to believe that you've never asked a man out."

"I have asked men out before," Gillian admitted. "But it's different this time. This time it feels like it really matters. Know what I mean?"

Hannah nodded. "And that's exactly why you need to do it."

Gillian bit her lip. "But—what if he says no?"

"You'd rather go through life not knowing if Lukas is the one than take that chance?" Hannah asked.

THE NEXT MORNING, Gillian was still searching for the answer to Hannah's question. In fact, she'd lain awake most of the night with the idea of asking Lukas out on a date banging around in her head like a pinball machine that didn't know the meaning of the word *tilt*.

"What do you think, Pirate?" she asked the cat while she finished dressing. "Should I take a chance?"

Pirate closed his eyes, raised a paw and started to lick.

"I know, I know. You're bored with the subject." She had, after all, been talking to the poor cat half the night about the situation.

"But it's different for humans, Pirate. It's a lot more complicated than just sniffing someone's butt and going off to sit together on a windowsill in the sun. There are things at stake here. Like a girl's pride. If I ask Lukas out on a date and he turns me down, then what am I left with? Zero. That's what. Not even a distant dream that we might be right for each other."

Pirate started on another paw. Gillian sighed and walked over to look at her reflection in the mirror above Aunt Clemintine's dresser. Last night, Agnes Sheridan had said maybe she wasn't all that different from Clemintine, after all. Was it possible that, given the chance, Lukas might see what the old lady saw?

She made a face at herself. Nah. He thought she was a big-city brat. A spoiled princess who cared about nothing but her own ambition.

But she wasn't. He was wrong about her. Or maybe she had changed. Like Hannah said, Timber Bay did odd things to people.

Pirate hopped up onto the dresser, knocking a few makeup pots and perfume bottles over. Gillian picked him up and the old, scarred cat started to purr and rub his face against her cheek.

"I'm a fool if I don't try, aren't I?" she asked him.

"Meow," Pirate said. And then he did something he'd never done before. He fell asleep in her arms.

She carried him downstairs with her, laying him on one of the slipper chairs while she opened Glad Rags for the day.

After a few hours of waiting for customers that never appeared, Gillian was wandering around, straightening things that were already straight, wondering how she was going to get up the nerve to risk being rejected by Lukas McCoy, when a shadow fell across the floor. She looked up.

Lukas was standing outside the window, watching her. Her heart went a little crazy.

"Oh, my God," she murmured to Pirate out of the side of her mouth, "he's coming in."

Pirate hissed, jumped down from the chair, and wiggled under it just as Lukas opened the door.

"I know what you did," he said.

Gillian looked around the shop, searching for a clue as to what offense she might have committed this time. But when she focused back on Lukas, his face was soft—not at all accusing.

"I'm not sure what you're talking about, but I'll be glad to take credit for it if it was something good," she told him. After all, if she was going to go through with asking him for a date, she needed all the brownie points she could get.

"Hannah told Danny about your visit to Mrs. Sheridan—"

"And Danny told you," she finished for him.

He grinned and it was like a reward that she thought she'd never again receive.

"Gilly, when I heard, I just about burst. I thought you'd be dancing in the streets when you found out that Brunswick was taking over the hotel."

"So did I. But Lukas, when I found out they wanted to get rid of your banister—and that gorgeous ballroom— and then I remembered what you said about wood—and about how much you loved tradition. And then when Hannah told me that Agnes was being coerced—"

Lukas's grin deepened and Gillian forgot what she was going to say. Those dimples had rendered her speechless. She wasn't at all surprised when the spinning started.

But inside the tornado, Lukas was perfectly still, perfectly in focus. He touched her cheek with his fingertips while his gaze moved over her face. "Aw, Gilly," he murmured. Then he thrust his fingers into her hair, pulled her head back and lowered his mouth to hers. In a move so smooth she'd swear they'd done it a hundred times, he lifted her at the waist and she wrapped her legs around him.

"You feel even better than my memories, Gilly," he said between sweet kisses along her jaw. His tongue delved lightly into her ear and she gasped and thrust her hands into his hair, tangling her fingers into his blond curls. Now it was her turn to pull his mouth back to hers, thrusting her tongue deeply, feeling the moist, soft slide of his tongue on her teeth.

There was the sudden blast of a car horn from outside the shop and Gillian came up for air.

In the name of Versace, they were at it again! And during store hours, too.

"Put me down!" she demanded, while she frantically tried to see if there were any witnesses walking by.

"I knew it was too good to last," Lukas grumbled as he lowered her to the floor.

"This is insane," she said once her feet were back on the ground. "I mean, every time we're together it ends up in a clinch."

"Yeah, princess," he said as he scowled down at her. "I noticed. And believe me, it's taking its toll."

"What do you mean by that?"

"Huh! You gonna tell me you're not staring into the dark at night, thinking about what it's like between us?"

Oh, she was staring and thinking, all right. But it made no sense.

She took a deep breath, then asked, "What do you know about the legend of the Tunnel of Love?"

Lukas groaned. "Who's been talking?"

She shook her head impatiently. "Never mind that. Do you believe in it?"

It took a few seconds before he answered. "Well, it worked for Danny and Hannah. They had their first kiss in the tunnel and now they're married."

"So you believe in it?"

He shrugged. "Even if I did, we don't exactly qualify."

"Rumor has it that some of the denizens of Timber Bay think we do."

"Well, well, princess. I never figured you for believing in fairy tales."

Gillian flicked her head dismissively. "I don't. But how do you account for the fact that we always end up with our lips and bodies locked whenever we're together?"

Lukas looked confused. "So you *do* believe."

"I didn't say that. But this—this thing between us is bugging me enough to want to make sure."

Lukas frowned. "And how would we do that?"

Gillian chewed her lower lip in thought.

"Don't do that," Lukas said.

"What?"

"Chew your lip like that. Makes me want to kiss you."

"Oh," she said, and melted.

"And don't look at me like that, either."

Gillian shook herself. "You're right. Another clinch will get us nowhere. I propose that we should spend some time together."

"We've already done that, princess. Remember how it turned out?"

"No—I mean go out on a—um—" she grimaced, not at

all sure how he was going to react "—on a real date. You know—where we have to talk and stuff."

Lukas gave her a twisted grin. "And what's gonna keep us from ending up like we always do?"

The whittler had a point. She resisted chewing her lip over it. "Okay—what if we set some rules?"

"What kind of rules?"

"No kissing. No touching. And absolutely no loosening of clothing. We'll take sex completely out of the equation and see what we end up with."

"Okay, so that's what we *don't* get to do on this date. Now tell me what we *do* get to do."

Gillian shrugged. "You decide. Whatever kind of date you usually take a girl on."

Lukas thought it over. "Okay. Friday night, then."

She shook her head. There was no way she was going to lose another night of sleep over Lukas McCoy. "Tonight," she said emphatically. "Pick me up at seven."

"Seven it is," Lukas said with a grin.

When he left, Gillian was too distracted thinking of the night ahead to notice that Pirate had slipped out with him.

10

"EAT UP, TIGER," Lukas said as he set a small bowl of one of his mother's endless hot dishes on the floor. Tiger sniffed at it, then looked up at Lukas. "Sorry, buddy. I forgot to buy cat food."

Tiger took a taste, decided he could live with it, and dug in.

Yup, thought Lukas with a smile, things were definitely looking up. Not only did he have a date with Gillian Caine, but Tiger had come back. When Lukas had gotten home that afternoon, Tiger had jumped out of the back of the truck and walked into the house as though it was where he'd meant to live all along.

While Tiger ate, Lukas finished filling the old picnic basket he'd found in the attic when he'd bought the house. He added an empty, wide-mouth Thermos, grabbed his jacket, then headed out to his truck and drove to Sweet Buns.

While he watched Molly ladle soup into the Thermos, he asked, "Am I making a big mistake here?"

"Absolutely not," Molly said with mock horror. "My wild rice and mushroom soup is always the right choice."

"You know that's not what I meant. I mean, Gillian is probably used to fancy restaurants and men in suits. How can hot dogs on a stick and me in hiking boots measure up to that?"

Molly screwed the cover on the Thermos and tucked it into the basket. "The way I see it, Lukas, you've got to be yourself. That's the only way you'll know for sure if there could be something real between you. And believe me, you are wonderful just as you are. Gillian's a smart girl. She'll see it that way, too."

Lukas stood and picked up the picnic basket. "Thanks, Mol," he said. Then, because he loved her like the dickens but seldom really showed it, he leaned over the counter and kissed her on the cheek.

She dragged the towel from her shoulder and swatted him with it. "Go on—get out of here. Gillian's waiting for you."

Oh, man. *Gillian's waiting for you.* He liked the sound of that.

He stowed the picnic basket in the back of the truck, then lifted the huge birch branch he'd planned on giving her the night she'd gotten rid of her sling—and him. Was he being a fool to take it to her now? Maybe he should have gotten flowers. Maybe he should have made reservations at that new supper club in the next town.

Aw, hell. This was who he was. He held the branch aloft and headed across the street.

When she opened the door he held it out to her.

"Gee, McCoy. Most guys just bring roses."

Lukas grinned. What the heck. He liked her sass. "It's to replace the one I broke," he told her. "I thought you might still want to use it in the window sometime."

Surprise flickered in her big gray eyes. "You remembered," she said. "That's really sweet." She stepped back to let him in.

He propped the birch branch in the corner next to the worktable. There were sketches strewn across the table. He picked one up and studied it.

"That's just something I'm working on for Christmas," Gillian told him. "If I'm still here for Christmas, that is."

"Business still not good?"

"Worse. It's nonexistent. If the church ladies hadn't hired me to do their costumes for the Thanksgiving play, I'd already be gone."

And to think that once he'd thought that's what he wanted—Gillian Caine out of his life. "It's hard to start a business," he offered. "Danny and I had some real lean years when we started."

She shook her head. "I think you were right when you said that Timber Bay doesn't want to buy what I'm selling."

He couldn't believe that he'd said those words. They sounded cruel to him now. "I'm sorry. I never should have said that."

Gillian shrugged. "Truth hurts sometimes, but that doesn't mean it shouldn't be told."

He picked up another sketch. "Tell me about this one."

She moved closer to see what he was looking at. "Oh, that's a blast from the past. I remembered seeing mother/daughter dresses on relatives in old family pictures. I was thinking of resurrecting the idea. And that one," she said when he picked up another one, "is a preliminary sketch of a jacket I wanted to start working on for spring."

He watched her face as she talked, only taking his eyes off her when she gestured to something on the sketch. She caught him looking at her and said, "What?"

"Your mind never stops, does it? I bet you keep a sketch pad next to the bed."

She put a hand to her chest and gasped softly. "All my life, I've felt like nobody really got me. I mean, my parents always patted me on the head and sent me away to dream more of my girlish fantasies—like designing clothes was some phase I was clinging to because I was the only girl in the family—and the middle child besides. They've never understood that what I do isn't really a choice." She searched his face. "But you know, don't you?"

He nodded. "Sometimes it doesn't let you sleep. And when you do sleep, you dream about it."

"You see it in every leaf, in every flower petal—"

"In every grain of wood," he finished.

She smiled. "That's why I couldn't bear the thought of that beautiful banister being ripped out. I knew how you must feel about it."

They looked into each other's eyes and Lukas understood for the first time how much they were really alike. She had tried to rescue him just as he had always tried to rescue Danny.

"What you did was incredible," he said quietly.

"It was the right thing to do."

Her voice was soft and her big eyes glowed as she looked up at him. The urge to take her into his arms flooded him.

He cleared his throat and moved away from her. "We should get going."

"Right." She grabbed a jacket off the back of a chair.

"You're going to need something warmer than that." He looked at her feet. "And if you care if you get those boots wet, you better change them."

"How wet?" she asked. "It is November, you know."

He grinned. "Just a little wet, maybe."

"Okay—be right back."

"While you're at it," he called after her, "grab some gloves, too. And a scarf, if you've got one."

A few minutes later she clattered downstairs, wearing hiking boots, a Navy pea coat and carrying gloves and a scarf.

"This is all getting very intriguing, McCoy," Gillian said. "Where are we going?"

"I think I'll keep it a secret till we get there."

Gillian sat beside him in the darkened truck as he drove through town and down little streets she had yet to explore. Houses grew sparser and trees grew denser. Finally, Lukas turned onto a gravel road that cut through the trees. After a mile or so, the road ended in a small parking lot that fronted a beach. The bay, inky in the darkness, spread out before them.

Hmm, Gillian thought as she got out of the truck. The beach in November. Pretty original. Also pretty secluded. Despite what he'd said back at the shop about keeping to the rules, did he have seduction in mind? The place was lonely enough. But a little too cold. She buttoned her jacket, shoved her hands into her gloves, and wondered what his next move was going to be.

She watched him go around to the back of the truck and take out a rolled plaid blanket. He tucked it under his arm and she thought, *uh-huh.* Can't very well seduce anyone on the beach without a blanket. Especially in this weather. She was just considering whether she should remind him of the rules or play along and let him get a little further in his plan before she thwarted it when he pulled a huge wicker picnic basket and a kerosene lantern out of the back of the truck.

"A beach picnic?" she asked incredulously. "This time of year?"

"An old McCoy tradition." He lit the lantern, then reached in and turned off the truck's headlights. "There's a great spot, but we have to walk down the beach a ways."

Ah, she thought. So this is how he woos the local girls. She had to admit, it was original—and very romantic. No doubt there was wine or some other libation in the basket to aid her in forgetting the rules. Unfortunately, Lukas McCoy was in for a big surprise because she had no intention of forgetting the rules. She was determined to find out if there was anything other than sexual attraction between them.

"Here." He held out the lantern to her and she took it. He picked up the picnic basket and they left the parking lot and walked over the hard-packed sand.

They passed the dark silhouette of a closed refreshment stand. "Is this where you swam when you were a kid?"

"Sometimes. Mostly, Danny and I came here when the beach was closed for the year, deserted like it is tonight."

The waves crashed just inches from their feet and the wind tangled in her hair and stung her face. Out beyond the waves, the moon split the bay in half with a wide path of silver. "It's beautiful," she said.

"Are you warm enough?" he asked.

"I'm fine," she answered, trying to keep the smile from her face. This was how it would start. He'd offer to put his arm around her to keep her warm.

Only he didn't.

Gillian was still puzzling it out when they rounded a bend and entered a little cove that was protected by a rim of trees and shrubs. Aha, she thought when she saw that another blanket was spread out near a fire pit that had already been laid with wood.

She arched her brow at him and he gave her a twisted grin. "I came out earlier and got a few things ready," he said.

"So I see."

Lukas set the picnic basket on the blanket, then dropped to his knees beside it, patting the place next to him.

She crossed her arms. "Aren't you forgetting the rules, McCoy?"

He looked at her blankly. "I don't remember anything in the rules about hot dogs."

She frowned. "Hot dogs?"

He dug into the basket and came out with a package. He held it up. Hot dogs.

She wondered why she felt a little disappointed. What had she wanted him to pull out of the basket? Handcuffs and strawberry-flavored massage oil? Just so she could turn him down?

"I'll get the fire started."

Gillian wasn't much of an outdoors girl, but she had to admit that the beach in November held a certain charm. Especially if you had a big handsome lumberjack building your fire. She sat in the glow of the kerosene lantern and watched him while he worked. He was wearing a thick, creamy fisherman's knit sweater under his jacket, and jeans that were faded from wear instead of from a machine. When the fire caught, the flame danced across his blond curls.

Lukas added more wood, then stood and brushed his hands on his jeans. "I'll go find us a couple of long sticks to roast the dogs on."

He headed for the trees. Gillian warmed her hands at the growing flames while she gazed out at the bay and pictured a ball skirt in the darkest, inky blue with a sparkling silver sash tied at the waist, the tails floating down the side. All fluid movement like the water. And then, of course, she pictured herself in the ball skirt and held in Lukas's muscular arms as he twirled her around the marble dance floor at the Sheridan Hotel. Which only made her disgusted with herself. How was she supposed to get through a date with him without throwing herself into his arms? Weren't there any treaties anywhere outlawing cruel and unusual rules for dating?

The object of her fantasies came back with a couple of long sticks. He joined her again on the blanket and drew a Thermos out of the basket. When he opened it, the scent of rich coffee wafted out with the steam.

"Mmm. Molly's blend?"

"One of the perks of having a sister who owns a coffee shop," he told her as he poured her a mug.

A real mug, she thought approvingly as she took it and cupped her hands around it. "Have you and Molly always been close?"

He told her about his childhood and how Molly had been first a pest, then an ally. And how he loved Chloe to death. He told her about Danny and how one summer they'd built a fort in the woods behind them.

"We'd sit in there and plot what we were going to do with our lives."

"And did your plotting work out?" she asked.

He grinned. "Pretty much, yeah. What about you?"

"Are you kidding? Nothing has turned out as I've planned."

"Are you so unhappy here?"

She looked at him, surprised at the question. "No, I'm not unhappy here," she said, realizing that it was true. "I'm just afraid that I'm not going to be able to stay if business doesn't get better."

"There's still a chance Mrs. Sheridan will sell the hotel, you know."

Gillian gave a quick shake of her head. "But I don't want that. Not anymore. A chain would totally ruin that building. And the next thing you know they'd be putting in a fast-food place where the drugstore is."

Lukas groaned theatrically. "No more of Clara's grilled ham and cheese."

She laughed. "See? Disaster."

"But what about Glad Rags?"

Gillian shrugged. "I'm not saying that a national chain wouldn't have helped, but let's face it. It's the natives I have to turn into customers in order to make a living."

"You'll think of something," Lukas said.

She gave him a wry smile. "I hope so because it scares me to think about failing."

"Hey—where's that tough little girl that used to visit her Aunt Clementine?"

She raised her brows in surprise. "Tough? Me? I was never tough."

"Now who's kidding? I was scared to death of you when I was a kid."

She laughed. "That wasn't exactly the effect I was going for. But I guess it explains a few things."

"What do you mean?"

Shrugging, she said, "Oh, I don't know. I always felt I got sort of overlooked at home. There was just no room for a girl with all those boys. When I started coming to Timber Bay I thought I'd be the little girl from out East that everyone would want to know. I wanted everyone to think I was special." She shook her head. "I guess it backfired on me."

"I think a lot of kids thought you were stuck-up. To me, you were like something from another world."

She rolled her eyes. "Great. So you thought I was some kind of alien."

"No," Lukas said softly. "I thought you were the prettiest thing I'd ever seen."

Her heart gave a funny little lurch. "You thought I was pretty?"

The flames from the fire flickered over his face and danced in his dark brown eyes. "I still do."

The waves crashed on shore and the moon rode the water. If ever there was a moment, a place, a *man* that deserved a kiss, it was this one. Gillian waited for him to make a move. Waited? She *prayed* for him to make a move. Instead he cleared his throat and got to his feet. "Where are those hot dogs?"

He showed her how to whittle the stick to a point with a jackknife. He laughed with her when her first hot dog dropped into the flames and helped her spear the second more securely. They ate hot dogs right off the stick and drank coffee and talked. And when Gillian thought that she was colder than she could stand, Lukas helped her wrap up in the second blanket and produced another Thermos from the basket.

"Molly's mushroom wild rice soup," he said, then passed her some.

It was hot and fragrant and rich with butter and cream. "Your sister is a culinary genius and a genuinely nice person but she is going to single-handedly keep me from losing any weight."

"Women worry too much about their weight. You have a beautiful body," Lukas said.

She looked at him sharply, but he was spooning his soup calmly like he hadn't just said an extraordinarily wonderful thing. And he hadn't even been on his way to second base when he said it. It made her want to leap from the blanket and throw herself at him. Blasted rules. Gillian spooned in more soup and cast about for a safe topic.

In the sky above, the stars were even more beautiful than they'd been the night the tunnel had brought them together.

Yikes! She glanced over at Lukas. Was she starting to think that the mishap that had ended in a sprained arm qualified them for the legend? He looked over at her and she abruptly cast her gaze back up at the sky.

"Do you know anything about the stars?" she asked him.

"Nope. Stars always puzzled me. I can never see what they're supposed to look like—you know? Like I don't see a darn thing up there that looks anything like a bull or a hunter."

"Me, neither. I've always just made up my own names for the star formations I see."

Lukas chuckled. "I should have known. You use them the same way you use a bolt of cloth. Raw material for Gillian's own creations."

She laughed and the wind carried it off with the waves. "Tell me how you fell in love with wood."

They talked until the fire died to embers. Until the coffee was gone, all the soup had been eaten and the moon had gone to sleep for the night. They were lying on their sides, heads propped on their hands, facing each other.

Somewhere an owl hooted, the sound of it sharp enough to be heard over the waves.

She wanted to reach out and touch him. Just his face. Just his sweet, adorable face. But her pride wouldn't let her. If he could stand it, so could she.

Unless he wasn't even tempted. Was it possible? After what they'd shared those nights at the shop? Was this—horrible thought—*easy* for him?

"Come on," he said. "Let's put the fire out. It's getting late."

They doused the flames with water, then buried the site in the sand and headed back to the parking lot. Gillian had gloves on and was wrapped to her mouth in her scarf, but she wished instead it was Lukas who was keeping her warm.

They drove back to Sheridan Road in silence. At the door, he didn't even try to kiss her good-night. She felt unbearably weary as she climbed the stairs alone. She started looking for Pirate, then remembered that Pirate had taken a powder. Gillian missed him. She missed Lukas, too. What had she been thinking, making those stupid rules? She could be in his arms right now.

Or maybe not. Maybe Lukas wasn't in the least interested in breaking any rules. Like a disappointed kid, she stomped into her bedroom and started to undress, throwing her clothes around, pulling on a pair of old, faded flannel drawstring pants and a T-shirt that had shrunk in the wash. She had just dived under the covers when she heard a loud thumping. Someone was at the back door.

Her first thought was Pirate, but she didn't think his paws could make quite that much noise even if he *could* figure out how to knock. Whoever or whatever it was, they weren't going away. Throwing back the covers, she got out of the bed and tiptoed downstairs. She grabbed a yardstick off the table, held it over her head, and opened the back door a crack.

Lukas stood on the stoop. "I thought maybe we could go right on to date number two now," he said.

Gillian laughed and flung the door all the way open. He pulled her into his arms and kissed her exactly the way she'd wanted him to kiss her all evening long.

When his mouth left hers and he buried his lips in her hair, she murmured, "I thought maybe you didn't want me anymore."

He laughed and she felt the rumble of it against her breasts. "I just didn't want to be the first one to give in."

"We're a stubborn pair, aren't we?"

"Don't get me wrong—I loved being with you tonight. Talking with you. But lying there next to the bonfire, looking at you, I thought I'd burst from wanting to reach out and touch you."

"Touch me now," she whispered. And he did. He moved his hands over her back and down to her buttocks, fitting her tightly against him. And then his mouth came down on hers again. Long, slow, delicious.

Then all of a sudden, he pulled his mouth away. "You better tell me right now, princess, what the rules are for the second date."

She looked into his warm brown eyes. "No more rules."

"That's all I needed to hear." With his big hands at her waist, he lifted her. She wrapped her legs around him and he carried her upstairs and into the bedroom, lowering her onto the bed. The bedsprings creaked as he joined her.

He kissed her for a long time. Long enough to make her wet. Long enough to make her needy.

When his mouth left hers, he murmured, "I want to hear you." Then he slowly moved his hand down her body and cupped her between the legs.

She gasped. "No! Lukas—it will be over too soon."

"Hush," he whispered. "When it's over we'll just do it again." And then he started to move his palm on her and she threw her head back and let herself soar.

Lukas reveled in the noises that came from Gillian's mouth. She gasped. She moaned. She made little squealing noises and very unladylike grunts. Her breasts moved gently beneath her little T-shirt as she writhed. He could see her nipples, hard and erect, through the thin fabric and he groaned. He bent his head and nuzzled them, then he pushed the shirt up, baring her, running his hands over her. So soft. So full. He dipped his head and ran his tongue over her skin, tasting her. When he took her nipple into his mouth she gasped and bucked and he knew in that moment that he had to have more.

He stood and pulled his sweater over his head then tossed it aside. He shucked off his jeans. And all the while she watched him, her gaze moving openly over him. "Hurry," she said. That one word leaped through his body and made him throb. Lukas reached out and pulled off her soft flannel pants in one quick movement. And then, hard as he was, crazy as he was to be buried inside of her, he couldn't stop looking at her. The roundness of her breasts, the flare of her hips, her lush thighs. The warm, womanly place between them.

"When you look at me like that, you make me feel beautiful."

"You are beautiful," he told her.

Gillian held out her arms. "Come to me," she said.

She parted her legs for him and he lowered his body, bracing himself with his arms, and thrust into her.

Gillian cried out as he filled her and her body clenched itself around him. Her arms flailed out and she grabbed the bed spokes behind her and wrapped her hands around them, arching her back, as he plunged into her over and over again. Each movement sent a wave of pleasure through her, building, climbing, rocking her to the core. But when he bent his head and took her aching nipple into his mouth, she shattered completely. Trembling, she cried out, clutched at his shoulders with her fingernails. He threw his head back and groaned and she felt him burst inside of her. The heat made her climax again—and again.

When it was over, he was so careful of her, smoothing her hair back from her damp forehead, gently drawing her into his big arms. He held her for a long time, his thumb brushing her shoulder languidly, his heartbeat wild beneath her cheek.

When his heart slowed and his breathing grew more regular, she thought he'd fallen asleep. Until he whispered her name. "Gilly? Do you think it's the legend?"

She thought for a moment, then murmured, "Does it matter? All I know is I've never felt this way before."

"Never?"

Had she ever felt this way with Ryan? In the beginning, Ryan had been exciting. He'd opened up a new world for her—a world she thought she wanted. Now she didn't see how she could have ever wanted that world—or Ryan. And she knew for certain that she'd never, ever felt this way.

Gillian looked up at Lukas. "Never," she whispered.

She felt the breath of his relief go out of him. "If you hadn't said that, I don't know what I would have done."

"Shhh," she murmured, stroking his chest as she cuddled into him. "Go to sleep."

"I can't. I'm afraid you'll disappear."

She laughed softly. "This is my apartment, remember? I'll be here when you wake up."

"Promise?"

"Promise." A few minutes later he was asleep. She listened to him breathe and felt the steady beat of his heart under her hand. Even in sleep, he held her tight.

She'd never felt so special in her life.

An hour or so later, Lukas woke and she was still beside him. He roused her from sleep with his hands on her body and made love to her again, more slowly this time. Like they had the rest of their lives.

"YOU CALL THIS BREAKFAST?" Lukas asked as he looked at the big can of chocolate pudding in the middle of the kitchen table.

"Hey, it's got milk in it—and it was on sale."

Lukas laughed. "I bet you don't even know how to cook eggs, do you, princess?"

She grinned. "I know how to break them," she said before she spooned in another mouthful of chocolate pudding. "I do know how to cook oatmeal, though. Want some?"

He made a face. "I hate oatmeal. Clara down at Ludington Drugs fries a mean egg. Come out to breakfast with me."

She shook her head. "There's enough speculation about us already."

"Then walk me downstairs, at least." He held out his hand.

At the back door, Lukas took her into his arms. "I don't want to scare you away or crowd you or anything, but there's something you should know. I think I'm in love with you."

Gillian reached up and ran her hand down the side of his face, caressing a dimple with her fingertip. "Want to hear something even scarier? I think I'm in love with you, too."

He grinned. Those dimples, she thought—those dimples are *mine*.

"Can I see you tonight?" he asked.

"You better."

"Come see my house. I'll cook for you."

She ran a hand up his hard, broad chest and curled it around his neck. "All this and you cook, too?" she asked, arching a brow.

He laughed and blushed and she thought that she could get very used to a man who was big enough to carry her around but still sweet enough to blush.

Lukas gave her a quick, hard kiss. "Come at seven, okay?"

"Yes," she said.

When Gillian closed the door, she wondered how she was going to make it through the next nine hours.

11

"WHY DIDN'T I put in a new kitchen floor?" Lukas asked Tiger. In a show of obvious support, the cat stretched out on the old linoleum and closed his eyes.

"Yeah, that's true. It serves its purpose. But it sure as heck isn't good enough for Gillian Caine."

And neither, all of a sudden, was the pot of beef stew bubbling on the stove. Or the jug on the kitchen table full of mums he'd filched from the grounds of the hotel. He went through the dining room, messy with tools and lengths of wood, and into the empty living room. Why in heck hadn't he bought a sofa, at least? As it was, the room was bare, with nothing but the gleaming refinished oak floor to its credit. Gillian was going to take one look at this place and head for the hills when what he really wanted her to do was head for upstairs so he could show her the bedroom that would be theirs. So he could make love to her in the bed that they would one day share.

Yeah, Lukas thought as he headed back to the kitchen, he was moving fast. But in a way he'd known Gillian practically his whole life. He didn't see the point in wasting any more time. He wanted Gillian to be his. Now.

Back in the kitchen, he stirred the stew again, then set the table with mismatched bowls, silverware and a basket of rolls. He was wishing he'd bought new dishes when he heard the front door open.

"Anybody home?" she called and he forgot about the dishes and rushed to meet her.

Gillian was standing in the living room—*his* living room—looking beautiful in jeans and a sweater and holding a large tote bag.

"This floor is beautiful," she said. When she looked up at him her gray eyes were shining. "Your house is just gorgeous."

Lukas grinned. "You really like it?"

"Absolutely. The outside is adorable."

"You're adorable," he said, then grabbed her and gave her a quick kiss. "I was a little worried that it might be—"

"Stop worrying," she said, "and kiss me again."

He did. Longer this time. Deeper. Until Tiger meowed and wound himself around their legs and Gillian pulled away and looked down.

"Pirate!" she exclaimed. "What on earth are you doing here?"

"That's Tiger. Who's Pirate?"

"*This* is Pirate," Gillian bent and scooped up the cat, "my cat."

"Nah, that's Tiger. *My* cat."

"There couldn't possibly be two cats who look like this one," Gillian said as she nuzzled his furry neck. "He's been living with me for weeks, but he disappeared yesterday morning."

"He used to hang around the hotel. I fed him tuna sandwiches from Ludington's. And then one day he just disappeared. I've been looking for him for weeks. Then yesterday, when I got home, he hopped out of the back of my truck. He's been making himself at home here ever since."

Gillian smiled up at him. "Looks like we both own the same cat."

Lukas grinned. He liked the idea of that. "Guess we'll

have to work out some sort of living arrangement that will make all three of us happy." He took the cat out of Gillian's hands and set him down. "Scoot, Tiger. We've got some negotiating to do."

"His name is Pirate," Gillian insisted, looking adorably stubborn.

He put his hands at her waist and pulled her to him. "Tiger," he said. "Now let's get back to more important things." He kissed her again, but she was still holding on to the tote. "Why don't you put that thing down."

"Oh! That reminds me. Wait till you see what I've spent the day making."

She took the tote into the dining room and started unpacking its contents on his makeshift worktable. There was a green ruffled apron decorated with a coffee cup appliqué and a green gingham dress.

"Hey, those are Sweet Buns' colors."

"I made them for Molly. Do you think she'll like them?"

"Are you kidding? She'll love them."

"I've been working on sketches all day of things I think might bring customers into Glad Rags. I thought I could use Molly as my guinea pig."

Lukas pulled her into his arms again. "Hey, I'm available for experimentation, too."

"I'll keep that in mind," she said as she grinned up at him.

He was just about to kiss her again when the phone rang. "Damn. Come into the kitchen with me while I get that."

In the kitchen he picked up the phone. "Hello?"

"Agnes Sheridan wants to see us right away," Danny said on the other end.

"You mean now?"

"Right now. I think she's made her decision. I'll meet you at the estate in fifteen minutes."

"I'll be there," he said into the phone, then hung up.

"Trouble?" Gillian asked.

"That was Danny—" he paused and ran a hand through his hair as he wondered how Gillian would take the news. Best to just say it. "Agnes Sheridan wants to see us right away."

"Oh, Lukas. Do you think she's decided what she's going to do about the hotel?"

"That's what Danny thinks."

"Well, what's the matter? You don't seem very excited about it."

"To tell you the truth, I don't know what to hope for anymore." He hated the thought that what was best for him and his business could hurt Gillian and hers.

She took his hand and led him to the front door. "Hope for the same thing I'm hoping for, Lukas. Hope that Agnes Sheridan tells her grandson to go to hell."

"Aw, Gilly." He bent to kiss her. "I'll make it as short as possible. Will you wait for me?"

"Of course," she said.

After he got into his truck, Lukas looked back at the house. She was standing in the doorway, just like he'd imagined she'd been the night she'd gotten her sling off. That night hadn't ended so well. But this one would, he thought as she waved goodbye. This night was going to end with her in his arms.

After she shut the door, Gillian went back to the kitchen and peeked inside the pot on the stove.

"Hmm, beef stew." And judging from the aroma, very good beef stew. She picked up the wooden spoon on the counter and gave it a stir, then put the cover back on. "What do you think?" she asked Pirate, who was watching her. "Do you like it here?"

Pirate meowed. He was generally stingy with his meows so Gilly took it that he was very pleased. "I think I'd like it here, too," she said.

She plucked a roll from the basket on the kitchen table

and started to nibble as she wandered back to the living room. It felt so intimate to be alone in his house, waiting for him. Like a wife, she thought, grinning to herself.

The living room was beautifully proportioned, with a wide bay window that looked out onto the street and a fireplace with an oak mantel. There was a chess set on the mantel and she went over for a closer look. The pieces were little wood carvings of whimsical creatures of the like that Gillian had never seen before. "So this is what he's always whittling." She picked one up and studied it. If she ever doubted that Lukas qualified as an artist, the figure would have changed her mind. It was both intricate and imaginative. She placed it back on the board and turned to the rest of the room. It was bare of furniture which, to Gilly, made it a blank canvas that she couldn't help but fill. In her mind, at least.

She'd put a sofa over there, she thought. And a stuffed chair big enough for Lukas over there. And in the dining room—

She shook her head and grinned. "Getting a little ahead of yourself, aren't you Gilly?"

But it felt right somehow. This house. This man. She'd thought it would be a long time before she would trust any man ever again. But Lukas was so different from Ryan. Solid. Reliable. Loving. Kind.

She was in the front hall, gazing up the open staircase, when the phone rang. The machine picked up on the third ring.

"Lukas? It's Mom. Just wanted you to know that the Women of the Flock have gotten the first bill from Gillian. Rather than send it on to you, I figured you'd better give me the money and I'll pay it. That way there'll be no danger of Gillian finding out that you're the one who's paying for the costumes. I have to go out tomorrow afternoon but—"

Gillian listened to the message with growing horror.

When it was finished, she pushed the play button and listened to it again just to be sure.

"Of all the manipulative, conniving..." she muttered. "And I thought he was different." She started to pace. "I thought he was caring." She tore the roll in her hand apart as she paced—kitchen to dining room to living room and back again.

She was on the trip back to the dining room when the front door opened behind her. She whipped around. Lukas stood in the doorway, looking all boyish and charming and as American as apple pie. Only the package didn't hold apples this time. It held snakes.

"Great news," he said. "Agnes has called in some big gun lawyers. She's decided to fight Gavin. She says she's not giving up until she's in her grave. In fact—" He looked down and saw the crumbs. "You planning on losing your way?"

Gillian tossed the last of the roll in his face. "Don't you dare come in here all happy and cracking jokes and looking all cute!"

"Princess! What's the matter? After what you said before I left, I thought you'd be just as happy as I am about this."

"Don't you 'princess' me," she said as she stalked over to the answering machine in the dining room. "The cat is out of the bag, McCoy—in more ways than one." And then she pressed the play button on the machine.

As the message played, Lukas groaned and looked up at the ceiling. "Baby, I can explain."

"What's to explain? That my whole damn life from the Harvest Festival on has been nothing but a lie?"

"Baby, don't say that. I only did it because I didn't want you to fail."

"And you were so sure I would?"

"But—but—you had no customers—"

"So you decided to buy me some?"

"It wasn't like that. I was afraid you'd leave town—

and I didn't want that to happen. I hated the thought of you leaving."

"Gee, McCoy, here's an original idea—how about when you want something from a girl you ask her for it instead of going behind her back and manipulating her life?" Gillian jammed her fingers into her hair and held it back from her face. "I feel like such a fool! I mean, I'm the one who talked Agnes into fighting having that chain come in here just to help make your dream come true. And to think I consoled myself by reminding myself that at least I still had the contract to make those costumes. And now I find out that except for the clothes those two women bought— the two women who now have absolutely no reason to ever set foot in Timber Bay again partly because of me— and the dress I sold Molly at the Harvest Festival—" She stopped and stared at him. "*Oh, no*—don't *tell* me—" She already knew what the answer was by the look on his face. "You sent your sister over to buy that dress, didn't you?"

"Honey-bunch," Lukas cajoled. "I was only trying to help."

"Help? Wrong word, McCoy. Delete it and insert control, manipulate or dominate into the blank instead."

He spread his arms and showed just enough of his dimples to make him tempting—any other day of the week, that is. The fact that he was even a little bit tempting was only adding more fire to her anger.

"I really don't see what the big deal is, Gilly. You said you were enjoying being with the Women of the Holy Flock."

"That was *before* I knew that you were paying them off!"

He put his arms down and frowned. "Now you're talking nonsense, princess. Why don't we sit down and have dinner and then—"

"I'm not sitting. I'm not even staying," she said as she grabbed her purse off the kitchen table and headed for the front door. Along the way, she scooped up Pirate and tucked him under her arm. Lukas followed.

"Honey-bunch, come on."

She turned around and swung her shoulder bag dangerously close to his crotch. "Stay away from me, McCoy, or I'll bunch your honey for you good."

That stopped him. Nothing like threatening a man's prized possessions to make him back off, Gillian thought with satisfaction. "Where are you going with Tiger?" he asked.

"His name is Pirate—and I'm taking him home because he's mine."

"But Tiger belongs here—just like you do, Gillian. I—"

She slammed the door in his face and ran down the stairs to the car she'd borrowed from Molly. Gillian put Pirate in the passenger seat, then got in after him.

"You did want to come with me, didn't you?" she asked the cat.

Pirate curled up in a ball and closed his eyes.

"I thought so," Gillian said.

As she started the engine, she looked at the house. Lukas was lumbering down the steps, calling her name. She stepped on the gas. The tires squealed as she pulled away from the curb.

When she looked in the rearview mirror, Lukas was running down the middle of the road after the car.

She sniffled and swallowed the first of her tears. "How many guys would run after a car like that?" she asked Pirate. She shook her head sadly. "So much potential. Why did he have to turn out to be just as much of a snake in the grass as Ryan?"

Pirate raised his head and looked at her.

"All right." She sniffled again. "You're right. Lukas is a garter snake compared to Ryan's python. But I'm not getting into bed with any kind of snake ever again."

"I DON'T UNDERSTAND, Danny. I was only trying to help."

Danny shook his head and took a nail out of his mouth. "Women are a mystery, pal," he said.

Lukas watched his partner pound the nail into the crown molding they were installing in the hotel ballroom. Agnes Sheridan's new, high-priced lawyers had told her that Gavin didn't have a leg to stand on so they were back on the job. But he was having a hard time keeping his mind on work.

"She won't even talk to me," Lukas moaned from his perch on a second ladder. He fished a nail from his pocket and started to pound. "She won't pick up when I call. I went over to the shop but she wouldn't let me in. I tried to—ow!" he yelled as the hammer connected with the wrong nail. He stuck his throbbing thumb into his mouth and swore.

"Boy, you are in bad shape," Danny said.

Lukas took his thumb out of his mouth and shook it. "I barely slept last night."

Danny leaned his hip against his ladder. "If you keep this up, we're gonna have to register that hammer as a lethal weapon. Why don't you take a break? Go on over to Sweet Buns and get something to eat. Take your time. I can finish up here."

Lukas grudgingly agreed. When he walked into his sister's coffee shop, Molly was just hanging up the phone.

"Jeez, Lukas. What's going on with Gillian?"

"What do you mean?"

"That was Mom on the phone. Gillian just took the costumes for the Women of the Holy Flock over to the Walker house and dumped them on the porch. She told Kate they'd have to finish the costumes themselves because she didn't want any part of them."

Lukas slid onto a stool and buried his head in his hands. "I can't believe this is happening."

"You look like hell," Molly said.

She poured him a mug of coffee and set it down in front of him. The aroma revived him enough to pick it up and take a gulp. Molly, in an incredible show of sisterly love, didn't question him further until he was halfway through his second cup. Then he told her the whole story.

"I mean, I guess I can understand what she's feeling. But then why doesn't she fight it out with me? I'm in love with her, Molly. And she's in love with me. I know she is. So why isn't she giving us a chance to work this out? Why is she so willing to give up?"

"Because of Ryan," Molly answered.

Lukas looked up. "Ryan?"

"Oops," Molly said. "I gotta go do something in the kitchen."

Lukas grabbed his sister by the apron. "You're not going anywhere until you tell me who Ryan is."

Molly sucked in her lower lip before saying, "I promised not to tell."

"Please, Mol. Come on, I'm dying here."

She took a deep breath and blew it out with enough force to ruffle her bangs. "Okay—but only because you look so miserable. Ryan is the guy Gillian was involved with in New York. They were in business together—a boutique. Gillian was the designer and this Ryan was the business end. Gillian thought it was a partnership—that they owned everything fifty-fifty. But Gillian never paid too much attention to the business aspect because she figured they were going to end up married and it wouldn't matter."

Lukas did his best to ignore the jolt he felt at the idea that Gillian had been going to marry someone else. "Yeah—so what's that got to do with what I did?"

"Well, Ryan dumped her and she found out that everything was in his name. She had to walk away with nothing."

Lukas frowned. "I still don't see how—"

Molly rolled her eyes. "*Men*. Don't you see? In her mind, you were pulling strings behind her back just like Ryan did."

"But I was doing it to help her, not to swindle her!"

Molly shrugged. "Still strings, Lukas."

"She called me controlling," Lukas mumbled as he tried to puzzle it out. It still didn't make sense to him. But, hell, he was no expert on women.

"Well, there you go. She's looking at what you did as controlling."

"Manipulating?"

"Yup. And I'm not saying that she isn't overreacting— I'm just saying that I bet that's where she's coming from."

Lukas scrubbed his hand over his face. "Well, what am I supposed to do about it?"

"Why don't you give her a few days, Lukas? Let her calm down. Then try to talk to her again."

GILLIAN HADN'T OPENED the shop for three days. Why bother? Of course, she hadn't done anything else for three days, either. When she finally went down to the workroom, the sketches for the *Cocooning Accessories* line she'd been working on were strewn around like relics from another life. A life she thought she'd been building.

Besides the apron and cotton wrap dress she'd left at Lukas's house, she'd done sketches for a line of fleece and a line of bathrobes.

"Idiot," she muttered. She'd even been planning on calling the fleece *Timber Bay Wea*; she'd felt so good about the town and about Lukas and about—about her future, damn it! She gathered up the sketches and tossed them into the trash basket, then marched out into the shop. It was time she started packing things up. She was going home.

Two hours later Gillian had only managed to fill one carton. It wasn't her fault. It was the damn candy bars. When she'd started to pack up the lingerie, the black lace thongs sent her running upstairs for her stash of candy-aisle nutrition. Since she'd soon be eating her mother's pot roasts and hot dishes, there was no longer any reason not to binge. And she couldn't very well pack with chocolate all over her fingers, could she? Or with tears blurring her eyesight.

She sank into one of the slipper chairs, then immediately jumped up again. It was *the* chair. The one that—she sank into the other chair and started to unwrap another bar. But before she could take a bite, the phone rang. She didn't know how to answer it, so she just said, "Hello?"

"Hey, Gillian. This is Ina Belway."

"Oh—hi, Ina."

"I saw that stuff you made for Sweet Buns and I was wondering—"

"Wait a minute—you saw it?"

"Yeah. Molly was wearing it."

"Oh." Lukas must have given Molly the apron and dress.

"I was wondering if you'd do something like that for the tavern. Not as frilly, of course, and I don't want a dress. Maybe one of those carpenter-apron things with a hamburger where you put the coffee cup."

"Um—Ina—I'm—" Gillian stopped. She felt far too weary to explain to Ina that she was leaving and why. "Look, let me call you back on this, okay?"

After she hung up, she decided that packing up the workroom might be less emotional than packing up the clothes. She'd just started to sort through some papers when the phone rang again. This time it was Clara from the drugstore, asking about uniforms for the lunch counter.

"I'll call you back on that, Clara."

Next, Kate called and wanted to know if there was any chance she was going to be doing any gardening accessories. Gillian was starting to get a little suspicious. But when a restaurant in the next town called about aprons, she smelled conspiracy.

"How stupid does he think I am?" she muttered, heading for the front of the shop. She unlocked the door and flung it open. It crashed satisfyingly into the wall. She left it open and marched across the street and up the steps to the hotel. The front door was unlocked. Danny was in the lobby.

"Where is he?" Gillian demanded.

"In the ballroom," Danny said.

"How dare you do it to me a second time!" Gillian said as she burst through the French doors.

Lukas looked down from his perch on a ladder. "Gillian!" he exclaimed, his mouth starting to go into a grin before it died into a frown. "What are you talking about? Do *what* to you?"

"Don't play dumb with me. I've had four calls in the past hour from people interested in the things I made for Molly."

He did grin then. "Four? But that's great!"

She wanted to swat those adorable dimples off his face. "And what happens when you run out of money, McCoy? Where do I get my business then?"

"Wait just a darn minute, princess. You think that I'm behind this?"

"That's exactly what I think."

"Well, I'm not."

"Right. This is only a coincidence, huh?" He shook his head and she crowed, "Aha! So you're admitting you're behind it!"

"What I'm saying is it's no coincidence," Lukas said as he climbed down the ladder. "The stuff you made for Molly was great—she's been wearing them at the coffee shop for the past couple of days. Everybody who comes in loves them. Princess," he said when he was standing before her, "the fact is, you hit on something that Timber Bay will buy. It's your talent, Gillian, that had them calling. It had nothing to do with me."

Could he be as innocent as he looked and sounded? She was still trying to figure it out when there was a loud meow. Pirate was standing in the doorway.

"Pirate!" Gillian said.

"Tiger!" Lukas said at the same time.

Gillian turned to glare at Lukas and in that instant, Pirate disappeared. She went after him. Lukas followed.

"Pirate, stop! Come back." Then, over her shoulder, "I am not losing that cat again, so don't even think about keeping it if you find it first."

"Why can't it be *our* cat?" Lukas asked.

"Because you're a rat," she answered.

The cat led them through the dining room and the kitchen, then slipped through the partially open basement door.

Gillian threw open the door the rest of the way and followed. Lukas clattered behind her.

"He's heading for the tunnel," he said.

Gillian followed the cat into what looked like a wine cellar.

"Tunnel my eye. The cat is looking for something to go with fish. Maybe a nice Pinot Grigio?"

But the cat ignored the wine and started scratching on another door.

"You know, Tiger," Lukas said, "I think you might have the right idea."

Gillian watched as he took a key from a shelf and unlocked the door. Pirate scampered through.

"What did you do that for?" Gillian cried. "I told you that I'm taking that cat home with me."

"I did that," Lukas said, "so that I can do this." He scooped Gillian up, threw her over his shoulder, and followed Pirate through the door.

"Put me down, you big lug. What do you think you're doing?"

As Lukas carried her, the rectangle of light that was the door got smaller and the darkness settled all around them. Her heart was going wild. "Put me down, you brute, right this instant!"

And Lukas put her down.

But it turned out Gillian wished he hadn't. It was so dark, she couldn't even see what she was standing on. She reached out and grabbed hold of Lukas's shirt. She was clutching it in her hands when he struck a match and lit a lantern that was hanging on the wall.

She let go in a hurry. "Look, you better use that lantern to light our way out of here right now," she demanded as she looked wildly around at her surroundings, "or I'm going to—" The threat turned into a gasp. The walls of the tunnel were covered with paintings of vines and flowers. "What is this place?"

"This is Timber Bay's Tunnel of Love," Lukas answered.

It was beautiful. Magical. A place that was meant for people to fall in love. So what on earth was she doing here with Lukas McCoy?

"Get me out of here!"

"Not until you listen to reason. Maybe what I did was wrong—but I did it for the right reasons. I did it to help you—and I did it because I love you. I'm nothing like Ryan."

Gillian gasped again. "How did you—*Molly!* What are you guys, the rat family?"

"Molly just wanted to make me understand why you reacted the way you did. Something that you should have told me yourself."

She set her lips in a firm line and crossed her arms. Okay, maybe the big lug had a point. "That doesn't prove that you aren't behind the calls I got today."

"Maybe it doesn't. But I'll tell you something, princess.

If I had thought of it, maybe I would have done it—despite the fact that I knew you'd get even madder at me. Because I love you and I would do anything to get you to stay in Timber Bay. Even if it means keeping you captive down in this tunnel until the legend can take hold once and for all. So in the interest of time, and because I haven't slept a decent hour since you stormed out of my house, why don't you just tell me what it would take for you to trust a man again."

"As opposed to a miracle, you mean? Let's see—" Gillian started to pace, but since she was determined to not venture out of the circle of lantern light, it wasn't very effective. "For starters, a contract making us equal partners—I own half of your business, you own half of mine."

Yeah, like a man would fall for that.

"Done," Lukas said.

She stared at him. "Are you crazy? That would mean we'd be stuck with each other, no matter what."

"But that's exactly what I want, Gillian. To be stuck to you for life. If you love me, that is."

"Of course, I love you," she said without thinking. "That's not the point."

"Then what is?" he asked quietly.

Suddenly she felt something furry against her legs. She was about to let out a screech when she looked down. Pirate was doing a figure eight around their feet. And he was purring.

"He hardly ever purrs," Gillian said.

"I guess he likes seeing us together. How about it, Gillian? Want to make Pirate happy?"

Lukas had called him Pirate, not Tiger. It wasn't much to go on, but a girl had to have some faith. But she also had to cover her well-dressed butt.

"Do I get to pick the lawyer to draw up the contracts?"

"No problem."

"And do I get to dictate the terms?"

"Yup," he said, then put his hands on her waist.

"And do I get to pick the colors for the kitchen?" she asked as she placed her hands on his big, wonderful chest.

Lukas grinned and pulled her a trifle closer. "Whatever you want."

She skimmed her hands up his chest and around his neck, drawing his head down to meet hers. "Then I think we might be able to do a deal," she said.

"Then let's kiss on it," Lukas said. And they did.

AFTER SEVERAL MEETINGS with Philo Hernshaw, Gillian and Lukas chose to announce their engagement at the dress rehearsal for the Church of the Holy Flock's annual Thanksgiving Day play, where, Gillian was happy to discover, Mrs. Sheridan's pilgrim costume fit her like haute couture. The Women of the Flock were jubilant over the announcement. The tunnel, they said, had proven itself once again.

But a scarred old tabby with half a tail knew the truth. This time the tunnel had needed a little help to get the job done.

ATHENA FORCE

The Athena Academy adventure continues....

Three secret sisters
Three super talents
One unthinkable legacy...

The ties that bind may be the ties that kill as these extraordinary women race against time to beat the genetic time bomb that is their birthright....

**Don't miss the latest three stories
in the Athena Force continuity**

DECEIVED by Carla Cassidy, January 2005

CONTACT by Evelyn Vaughn, February 2005

PAYBACK by Harper Allen, March 2005

**And coming in April–June 2005,
the final showdown for
Athena Academy's best and brightest!**

Available at your favorite retail outlet.

Curl up and have a

Heart *to* Heart

with

Harlequin Romance®

Just like having a heart-to-heart
with your best friend, these stories
will take you from laughter to tears
and back again. So heartwarming
and emotional you'll want to
have some tissues handy!

Next month Harlequin is thrilled to bring you
Natasha Oakley's first book for Harlequin Romance:

For Our Children's Sake (#3838),
on sale March 2005

Then watch out for....

A Family For Keeps (#3843),
by Lucy Gordon, on sale May 2005

Available wherever Harlequin books are sold.

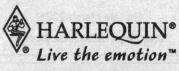

HARLEQUIN®
Live the emotion™

www.eHarlequin.com

HRHTH